The Shimmer

Dedication

This book is dedicated to everyone who has had to bravely navigate trauma, destruction, and the death of loved ones. Sometimes, vulnerability is much harder. Let love in.

I want to give big hugs and appreciation to Angie and Heather, who helped me prepare this book for publication. As you know, this one was a struggle from start to finish.

About the Series

There is no place more beautiful to me than the home I've made with the love of my life. We're surrounded by rushing waters, rugged landscapes, rolling hills and magnificent views. Where people are real, and life doesn't have to be perfect to be wonderful. It's the most magnificent inspiration for love. Inspired by the communities that form the Headwaters, the 'Love in the Hills of the Headwaters Series' will bring you stories you can relate to; people you can connect with; and love you can believe in. It's the perfect place for city glam to meet country charm. Come Join us in the Hills of the Headwaters and find a place to explore, unplug and fall in love.

The Shimmer- Prologue

Things change. People change. Relationships… change. Sometimes you see it coming. Sometimes you don't. This time, I was blindsided. I lock strong emotions deep inside as I watch the man I thought I would spend the rest of my life with pack half our belongings into a rented truck. He latches the door securely and then turns to see me watching from the door. I place my hand on the doorknob, preparing to join him in the front yard for dramatic last words before he drives away. Instead, he waves once in a casual goodbye and departs as if the four years of our life together meant nothing to him.

My parents have been waiting in the kitchen to provide moral support. My father scowls while reading the letter my ex handed me when he arrived. He lowers the letter and looks at me over the brim of his reading glasses as I enter the room. "He wants to sell his half of the house."

My mother looks sympathetic, and I avoid eye contact, hoping to suppress the emotional outbreak lurking below the surface. "How long do I have?"

"You have thirty days to arrange an independent real estate appraisal to ensure the value his agent has suggested is appropriate, and then you'll have the opportunity to buy him out."

I lean against the counter, feeling defeated. "Or sell and give him his money."

Knowing I will never be approved to carry the entire mortgage alone, he regretfully nods.

My parents are humble, hard-working people who saved every penny they could on a janitor's salary to put me through college. They wanted a big family, and my mother never gave up hope after many years of trying. Later in life, she thought she was going through early menopause when the doctor confirmed that she was pregnant with me. I am the blessing they never thought they'd have; all they want for me is happiness.

I stand silently, feeling gutted, as I recall how shocked I was when he told me he had fallen in love with someone else and was moving out.

My mother wraps me in a hug as tears trail down my cheeks, and I give in to the overwhelming sorrow I feel. "We'll help. As much as we can." She turns and locks eyes with my father in a silent plea for confirmation. "Stanley? We can help, right?"

My dad's expression is tortured. He feels every ounce of my heartache. "We'll find a way," he assures us both.

I wipe the tears from my eyes as I struggle with the sadness of my failed relationship. I shake my head. "This is my mess, and I won't let you sacrifice everything you've worked for and give up your retirement dreams."

My mom gives me a small, appreciative smile. "Then sell this place and come back home. You can live with us for as long as you want."

I hold back my initial response, not wanting to hurt her feelings. My dad looks at his watch. It's a silent signal to my mother that it's time to leave, and she immediately picks up her purse and buttons her sweater. I have no idea if it's because it's getting close to his dinner time, or maybe he doesn't want to miss his favourite television game show. I walk them to the door and say goodbye with a brave face so my mother doesn't feel guilty about leaving.

After closing the door behind them, I plop myself into the oversized armchair in the front room and try to disappear into its vast, fluffy cushions. Since I was a girl, I dreamed of a small outdoor wedding and a happy life in a home with white picket fences and many babies. I try not to reflect on the years of failed relationships and heartbreak, but I can't help but wonder if I'm doing something wrong. The thought of moving back home makes me feel like I've failed at adulting. I will admit that life was much simpler the last time I lived there. I credit that to my best friend and next-door neighbour, Sawyer Kelly. We instantly hit it off because we shared the same quirky humour. He was the boy who defended the underdog and rescued lost kittens. He would have been every girl's knight in shining armour in elementary school if it weren't for his awkward social skills—another thing we had in common.

In those uncomfortable high school years, we were each other's wingmen, even though neither one of us actually dated anyone. We kept each other company and became the other's 'pity' date whenever a party or social event required a plus one. With Sawyer, everything was easy. Everything made sense. When college started, we chose our career paths, met new friends, and slowly drifted apart. Since then, my adult life has been a whirlwind of impulsive decisions. Failed career choices and disastrous relationships have left me feeling discombobulated.

Maybe the only way to get back on track is to let go of this house and start over. Sawyer moved out of the province after college, but maybe some of his mojo still exists in the neighbourhood. I'll sleep on it, and unless I come up with indisputable reasons why I shouldn't move home, I'll call them in the morning and let them know I'll accept their offer until I get back on track.

Chapter One

Two Years Later…

When I agreed to move back with my parents, I didn't intend it to be long-term. I never thought in a million years that my mother would pass away from a sudden heart attack shortly after I moved in. It crossed my mind more than once that the universe had it all planned out, and I was meant to be here for my father when it happened. My mother was a strong woman. Had it happened the other way around, and my father passed away first, she would have persevered. My dad was devastated. He puts on a brave face for my sake, but I can tell her passing extinguished the light inside him. If I weren't here to see him get up every morning and get dressed, I'm sure he would stop living and fade away until he joined her.

He shuffles past me in the kitchen, looking like he hasn't had a moment's sleep since she passed. At least today, he got dressed on his own.

"Good morning, Dad." I place a bowl of cereal on the table in front of his spot. I try not to let my frustration show when he greets me with nothing but a nod. "What are your plans for today?" I ask.

His hand trembles slightly as he lifts the spoon to his lips. "The same thing I do every day."

"Sit in the garden and watch the birds?" I pause and wait for a reply, but he ignores me and stares aimlessly into his bowl. I sigh. Sometimes, it feels like I lost both parents that day.

"I like to watch the hummingbirds." He dabs his chin to soak up the milk that dribbled off the shaking spoon.

"They were Mom's favourite," I acknowledge as I look at the time on my phone.

He nods. "She believed they are messengers from heaven, and the spirits of our loved ones who have passed away travel with them."

I can hear the emotion in his voice, so I stand behind him and place my hands on his shoulders to comfort him. I'm aware of my mother's belief in the symbolism of the hummingbird. Their message to *live in the moment and enjoy life's simple pleasures* is not heard by my father these days, yet I still try to encourage him. "Ancient natives believe that a hummingbird crossing your path means you're on a journey, and by the end, you will develop the strength and courage to endure." I place my lips on his head, wishing I felt more hopeful. "I need to leave for work now. Enjoy your day."

As always, I hesitate at the door, worrying that today's the day he will need me, and I won't be here. I carry that anxiety with me every day at work. On the way to my car, I glance at the house next door as laughter erupts from small children playing in the driveway. It takes me back to simpler, happier times when Sawyer and I spent endless hours playing hopscotch. As I drive to work, the sun shines brightly through the car window, creating warmth on my face, but my heart still feels heavy as I park in front of the stone heritage building where I'm the part owner of a business. It's a short walk up a cobblestone pathway, and then I take a deep breath and exhale the negative energy as I open the main door to the small store. I need a clear head to get through my day. As I flick on the lights in the room in the back that I use as my office, the sound of "Good morning!" echoes from the shop.

"Good morning!" I call back. "Why are you working in the dark?"

My business partner, a robust, middle-aged woman, appears at my office door with a steaming cup of coffee. "I don't mind working in the dark. It's peaceful." She hands me the cup and smiles. "How was your weekend?"

I frown. "The same as every other weekend. Boring."

"My nephew has a friend who just moved back to town."

"NO!"

"Don't be so quick to turn me down. He's a smart, handsome lad. He was offered a job out of the province right after college. He's been there for ten years and decided to return to Dufferin County recently."

"Bad break up?"

"Not as far as I know."

"Got caught cheating?"

She blinks her eyes rapidly. "As far as I know, he hasn't been in a relationship for quite some time."

My eyes narrow. "Why is he single?"

"I guess he just never found the right woman. His career took up much of his time, and he still does volunteer work."

I place the coffee on the desk in front of me. "Or he's a jealous control freak with disgusting sexual fantasies who lives with his mother and has never grown up, so he spends his nights playing video games in the basement."

Her face turns bright red, and I'm embarrassed by my outburst. An awkward tension fills the room as she retreats toward the door. "I'll check the phone messages before opening the store."

"Sara, wait! I'm sorry."

"All good," she calls back as she walks toward the merchandise storeroom. "I'm not giving up yet."

"That doesn't surprise me," I mumble as I scroll through the supply chain and accounting records. I recently moved to an online system for my sanity. As a small business that deals with repurposed and restored vintage pieces designed for our more modern clientele, we have a lot of single purchases from local artisans and vendors. We are thriving for the first time since we opened a year ago. The numbers begin to run together into an indecisive blob. I massage the stiffness out of my neck, working my way to my shoulder. My hand skims over the tattoo I got in college. Sawyer probably would have talked me out of it if he had been around. But I felt lost, and its symbol reflected hope and positive things to come. Happier times. It was a meaningful and powerful message for me until the universe dealt my hand from the bottom of the deck. My faith in its symbolism was somewhat fractured when my mother died.

The door opens, and Sara stands staring at me. "Are you okay?"

"Yes. Why?"

"You've been in here all day, and it's almost time to close. It's not like you to hibernate in here."

"Sorry, I'm fine. I got caught up going through the accounts payable records."

"Speaking of which, Jake McCarthy is here. Do you have payment for the stuff he brought in last week?"

I pick up a pile of envelopes and thumb through them, stopping at the one I need. I pull it out of the stack and hold it out in front of me. Sara gives me a small smile.

"Are you sure you wouldn't want to give it to him yourself?"

I roll my eyes and sigh. "Stop with the matchmaking."

She laughs and takes the envelope out of my hand. "You wouldn't be interested anyway. He lives with his father."

"That's completely different. He moved home to help look after his dad and the family farm. He didn't fail to launch or crash and burn."

She grins as she turns. "Neither did my nephew's friend," she adds as she walks away.

I rake my fingers through my hair and hold my head in frustration. The woman is exhausting. I glance at the time and power down my computer. She's right; it's time to close.

Every day brings extended periods of sunlight, signalling that summer will soon be upon us. My mind races as I walk to my car. Jake adjusts the load in his trailer and secures it tightly. He looks up and waves as I leave the parking lot. I nod and smile. He is a good-looking guy. If he is single, I'm sure he won't be for long.

I ponder my life all the way home. When I pull into the driveway, I glance toward the house where Sawyer and his parents used to live, and once again, I feel *lost*. It's dark out now, and the streetlights have come on. The children laughing and playing out front have long since gone inside.

I'm so tired that the short walk to the front door feels like a marathon. Feeling alarmed that the front door isn't locked, I rush down the hall to check on my dad, only to find him already retired for the evening and sound asleep. I wish I could think of a way to help him enjoy life again. Our home was bright and full of laughter and love; now, all that's left is a shell of the man he used to be when my mother was alive. The house is dark and quiet, and it fosters a feeling of loneliness.

After climbing into bed, I opened a novel and repeatedly read the same paragraph several times before accepting that I was too distracted and tired. I place it on the nightstand and glance at the time before turning off the lamp. I once dreamed about taking on the world, but instead, I'm in bed at ten o'clock. I'm struck by the realization of how quickly things can change from the grand plans.

Floorboards creak on the other side of the room for no reason at all. I've been experiencing strange sounds and shadows in the house lately. My dad would say it's an old house settling, but there have been times when I'm not so sure that's true. Tonight, I close my eyes and ignore it, giving in to emotional exhaustion. Within moments, I drift off to sleep.

Chapter Two

I lay awake under the covers, wondering how to help my dad enjoy his life again. When I get up and start my day, it consumes my thoughts while I fix his breakfast. As I put away the clutter that was on the counter, the magnets on the side of the fridge catch my eye. Each represents a treasured family trip we took together when my mom was still alive. I wonder if this could be the answer I'm looking for.

I take a cup of coffee to him, taking care not to spill it on the way to the garden. He doesn't acknowledge me as I sit beside him on the bench. "Dad, I was thinking about how you and Mom planned on using your savings to travel together when you retired. I think she would want you to go."

His brow lowers. "By myself?"

"Well, unless you have friends you'd like to travel with."

His eyes dampen with tears, and my heart sinks. That's not the outcome I was hoping for. I scramble to recover. "I could take some time off, and we could travel together."

He stares silently at the hummingbird feeder, waiting for a glimpse of one. Deep in my heart, I know he's hoping my mother's spirit will return to him and bring him joy and hope. I miss her, too, but he mourns that connection much more profoundly than I will ever truly comprehend. I abandon my efforts since it's clearly not the right time. "I'm going to the farmer's market behind the townhall building. Is there anything you'd like?"

"Raisin bread from the Mennonites."

"You bet. Please consider doing some travelling. We can talk about it at dinner."

A hummingbird sweeps in and hovers at the feeder before darting away quickly. "Dad?" I've lost him. I walk the pathway alongside the house and pause at the garden gate. I wonder if the day will come when I don't have a sense of impending doom when I have to leave. Today is not that day. I take a deep breath and continue to my car.

It's a short drive into town. I always take the back roads because I love to drive through the older parts of town with the beautifully landscaped gardens and well-looked-after heritage homes. I always park a few blocks away to avoid the gridlock that often happens on the small town's main street.

The fresh air is revitalizing, and walking along the closed roadways to shop at the many farm and artisan booths helps lift the heaviness from my spirit. I collect business cards from vendors whose beautifully handcrafted goods would fit well in our store.

I leave my food shopping until last, so I don't have to carry it around. Familiar laughter echoes in a nearby alleyway as I stand at a vegetable booth, trying to decide between green or yellow beans with supper. A nervous excitement rushes through me. It can't be him.

The woman beside me impatiently brushes against me, nearly toppling me over, as she grabs a pint of yellow beans. I give her an annoyed look and then stretch and strain my neck, trying to see through the holes in the canvas as the laughter gets closer. Curiosity has me on edge. I focus on the quart basket in front of me, waiting for him to walk past so I can get an unobstructed view. The vendor watches me intently as if I'm some lunatic with a green bean fetish.

I close my eyes, focus on blocking out all the extra noise, and listen for his voice. I step out of the booth and glance in all directions, but I can't see him in the crowd. Maybe I imagined it. For a moment, I thought I'd wished to have my best friend back so much that I had actually manifested him. Excitement quickly turns to disappointment.

I stop for tea on the way home, but the drive-thru window at the most popular spot to stop for a beverage and a snack is lined up around the parking lot. I knew the decision to park and go in would be an exercise in control, and it is. The lineup inside isn't much better, and since the staff prioritizes the drive-thru line, it probably would have been faster for me to stay in my car. Looking at the goodies on display has a huge impact on my buying impulses, and the longer I wait, the more I want to buy. I close my eyes and groan when I realize I'm going home without the one thing my dad asked for from the market.

As I walk back to the car, I'm trying to juggle my purse, tea, and the box of treats that I don't need and shouldn't have bought. I'm distracted as I struggle with yanking my keys out of my pocket without dropping everything.

"Do you need a hand?"

I stop walking and slowly raise my eyes. "Sawyer," I gasp. My heart pounds at the sight of him leaning casually against the hood of my car.

He grins as he nods. "Grace."

"What are you doing here?" With hands fully loaded, I move in for a hug.

"I thought I saw you at the farmers market, and then I stopped for gas, and there you were, heading into the coffee shop."

"It's been a long time. I'm surprised you recognized me."

He raises a brow. "It's been ten years. You haven't changed much since college."

I can't help but notice he's changed *A LOT* since college. I suddenly feel awkward and uncomfortable. I finally pull the keys from my jacket pocket and approach the door. "I'm sorry, but I have to get going, but it's wonderful to see you."

"Are you okay?" he asks concerned.

"Yes, fine," I insist as I pull on the handle. "My father is waiting for me to help with dinner."

"Here, let me hold that." He reaches for my tea, taking it out of my hand while I fumble with my key. Holding the top of the car door with the other hand, he stops it from closing while I get in. "How are your mom and dad?"

I toss the baked goods onto the passenger seat and try to hold off an emotional response. I frown. "Mom passed away almost two years ago. Dad's not coping so well."

"Oh, Grace. I'm so sorry. I didn't know, or I would have reached out." His masculine, husky voice takes on a caring and gentle nature. The nurturing tone promotes feelings of calmness and peace inside me. I've missed those feelings. I realize he's still holding my tea as I reach for the door handle and pull the door toward me. Feeling embarrassed, I open the window, and he passes me the cup with an amused smile. "I just moved back to town, and I'd love to get together and catch up."

"Sure, that sounds great." I pause for a moment and smile. I can't believe he's actually standing here. It's got my mind so distracted that I back up and pull away without first exchanging numbers. In the rearview mirror, I see he's watching me drive away. My heart squeezes painfully. This is precisely how it ended the last time I saw him.

There's no scenic drive home for me. I take the fastest route possible. I'm almost home when I remember about the raisin bread. I detour down one of the side streets and stop at the new local bakery. I avoid impulse buying this time and only grab what I'm there for.

"That's nine dollars," the teenager behind the counter announces.

My eyes open wide. "For what? I'm only buying one loaf of raisin bread."

"Yes, that's the price."

"For a loaf of raisin bread?" I repeat, gobsmacked. "Are you charging per raisin now?"

"No, ma'am."

And there it is…the grand finale to what has been a very eventful morning. *Ma'am.* Ugh. I pay and then grumble all the way home in the car.

My dad is sitting on the front porch when I get there. That's a welcome sight.

"How was your morning?" I ask as I reach the front door.

"It was good," he says cheerfully. "Did you get my raisin bread?"

"I did. Would you like some?"

"Lightly toasted, please."

"It's a nice day." I open the door. "I'll get us both some, and we can eat out here."

I lower the slices into the toaster and stare out the window at Sawyer's childhood home.

I'm so distracted by my thoughts that I jump when the toast pops. I butter the toast and go outside, laughing at how ridiculous I'm behaving. "Have you given any thought to doing some travelling?" I ask as I put the plate on the table beside him.

"I don't want to travel without your mother."

I frown. "Not even if I go? You wouldn't want to spend time with your only daughter?"

He ignores my question and picks up his raisin toast. I guess I'll change the subject. "Hey, Dad. Guess who I saw today?"

"Who?"

"Sawyer Kelly."

He narrows his eyes as if he's trying to remember the name.

"Sawyer Kelly," I repeat. "My best friend from next door."

"Oh," he says, resting the toast on the plate. "Tell him his father needs to trim that hedge along the garden path. It's getting too long and out of control."

Oh boy. I furrow my brow. "They don't live there anymore, Dad."

"They don't?"

"No, they moved a long time ago."

"Oh," he says, clearly confused.

Another subject change is in order. "Are you going to finish your raisin toast?"

"No."

"What? Why not?"

"It's not the same. You didn't buy that from the Mennonites."

My shoulders fall. "You're right. I stopped at the new bakery instead."

"It's horrible."

I laugh once. I could have saved myself nine bucks. Next time, I'll manually press raisins into an ordinary piece of bread. "Sorry, Dad. Don't eat it."

"I think there's a new box of chalk in the garage."

I cock my head to the side. "Why do I need chalk?"

"In case you and Sawyer want to play hopscotch."

My heart hurts a little. I pick up the plates and kiss him on the forehead. "Thanks, Dad."

"Anything for my little girl and her best friend."

I smile through the pain of knowing his reality is starting to slip.

"Hold the door, Gracie. I'm tired and think I might lie down for a bit."

"Sure, Dad." I help him to his room. "Is there anything I can get for you?"

"No. I need a quick cat nap."

"I'll check on you a little later. Do you want me to wake you for supper?"

"What are we having?"

"Definitely not nine-dollar raisin bread," I mumble.

"What was that?"

"Nothing. I'll check to see what's in the freezer." Suddenly, I hear the flutter of wings as something flies over my head. Startled, I duck. "What was that?"

"What?"

"Something is flying around. Is there a bat in the house?" My eyes scan the room.

"I don't see anything," my father says, looking around the room. "What did you see?"

"I don't know. It was too fast." I walk to the window and cautiously move the curtains, searching for the intruder. I hear fluttering behind me and turn quickly. "Where is it? Do you see it?"

"Grace. There's nothing in here."

I look around the room, feeling apprehensive. "Something was flying around here."

He holds his hands up in the air, proving his case. "Nothing. Have you been smoking that wacky tobacky with your friends today?"

I pause, then place my hand over my mouth, trying not to laugh. "Have a good rest, Dad." I close the door behind me and lean my ear against it, still on high alert. I know I heard something.

Chapter Three

My dreams are full of hummingbirds. Restlessly, I toss and turn because I see them every time I close my eyes. When the sun rises, I'm not sure I've had even a moment of sound sleep. Feeling perplexed, I sit on the bench outside facing the hummingbird feeder, and eat one of the sugary treats I bought yesterday. I've always been skeptical of my mother's belief in signs or spirits, but my dream was so vivid and compelling that I want to believe. I'm not sure what I expected, but nothing magical happens when I finally get a quick glimpse of a green-chested visitor. Feeling I've just wasted an hour for no reason, I decide to get on with the errands I need to run today.

An unseasonably warm day lends itself to a pleasant walk downtown Orangeville. Vendors and small shops have taken advantage of the weather to display their goods on the sidewalk. Our shop is in darkness. Typically, our clientele is more of a professional crowd. Home stagers and interior designers are the target market for our reclaimed and renewed treasures. When this location became available, we liked it mainly because the space was perfect and required very few changes, but it is an ideal downtown location for retail space. We are open to the public but have never opened on weekends because we can't afford to hire additional staff, and neither of us wants to work seven days a week. People stop on the sidewalk and strain to see what's inside the dark shop through the window. I can't help but feel we have a missed opportunity here.

I decide to stop for tea on the patio of a small café before I head back to my car. I'm completely lost in thought while sipping the soothing chamomile tea and watching the parade of vintage cars that have just been freed from winter storage proudly showcase themselves through town. A masculine hand reaches for the chair across from me and pulls it back, startling me with the scraping sound across the cement patio.

"Mind if I join you?"

I laugh once. There's no point in answering. He's already sitting down.

He places a steaming mug on the table. "Penny for your thoughts."

I can't help but smile. "I'm wondering why the great Sawyer Kelly is back in Dufferin County after all these years."

He smirks. "Life changes directions sometimes."

"That's very cryptic. Since when do you drink tea?" I mock.

He raises his brows defensively. "A man can't drink peppermint tea?"

"I've just never known *you* to drink tea."

"Well, I've matured."

I grin, and his face lights up. "There it is. That million-dollar smile I've missed so much. What are you doing now?"

I feel a great deal of pride. "I co-own a small design store in town. It specializes in reclaimed vintage pieces, repurposed salvage, and art."

His brow lowers as he tilts his head to the side. "Interesting. I never saw that coming. Did you ever leave town?"

I purse my lips and hesitate. "No."

He straightens in his seat. "What happened to your dreams of moving to the big city and bringing home a six-figure salary?"

I shrug and sip my beverage to hide my need to avert his judgmental glare. "Just like you said back then. It didn't end up being as important as I thought." I place my cup on the table in front of me.

He leans back in the chair with a victorious grin. "You stayed for a guy."

I roll my eyes. "Yes."

"That's wonderful. I'm happy for you."

"Not really. It didn't work out. He fell in love with someone else," I announce bitterly.

"He's an idiot, and you deserve much better."

I believe it when it comes from Sawyer. "What about you? Did you ever…"

"Settle down? No. I've never found the right girl." There's a ghost of a smile across his lips as his eyes lock on mine. The sudden warming of my cheeks brings awareness that I'm blushing—a reaction I wasn't expecting.

A sudden screeching alert comes from his phone, making us both jump. I try to steady my heart rate as he quickly shuts it off and reads an incoming message.

"I signed up to be a volunteer firefighter when I returned to town. I'm sorry, but they need me to respond to a call." He gets to his feet quickly, nearly knocking over the chair.

I smile as I stand. "You were always destined to save the world."

He pulls me into a firm hug and leans his cheek against mine. "It was nice running into you again. I still want to have dinner and do more catching up."

He practically bolts for the door, and as he disappears onto the street, I realize I still didn't get his number. Somehow, I know I'll be running into him again. For once, the universe seems to be working in my favour.

I smile the entire drive home. When I arrive, I find my father sitting in the living room dressed in his best clothes and looking content. "Hi," I say cheerfully. "It's nice to see you up and looking so handsome."

"I had a lovely visit with your mother today."

My brow raises. "You went to the cemetery on your own?" I ask, feeling concerned.

"Heavens, no. I haven't driven in over a year, and it's too far to walk."

I begin to feel anxious. "Did someone pick you up and take you there?"

"No, she was here."

"Who?"

"You're mother, Grace. Aren't you listening?"

I pause, unsure how to react. "Mom, came here? To the house?"

"Yes. She said she would come today, and she did."

I'm at a loss for a delicate way to say this, so I blurt it out. "Dad, Mom isn't with us any longer. She passed away, remember?"

"Isn't it wonderful? We watched the hummingbirds for the entire morning."

I nod, feeling emotional. I don't have it in me to rob him of this pleasant encounter, even if it's impossible. It's the happiest I've seen him in a long time, but I'm afraid he will mourn her loss even harder when the truth kicks in.

The first thing I did Monday morning was call our family doctor, and luckily, they had a cancellation. My father is being as difficult as possible, almost as if he knows. "Why are we here?" he demands loudly in the physician's waiting room.

"Just for a check-up, Dad," I reassure him. The nurse escorts us to an exam room, and as he sits and waits for the doctor to join us, I can see he's feeling uneasy. I hope I'm doing the right thing.

The doctor whips the door open quickly, startling us both. He clutches a clipboard against his chest. "Stanley. It's great to see you. This might be the last time I see you as your physician. I've finally decided to retire."

"Oh, no," I mumble under my breath.

"It's time," he assures me. "So, Stan. Why are you here today?"

"Oh," I intervene. "I thought the nurse might have mentioned why we're here."

He looks at the chart, flips a few pages, and then gives me a sympathetic look. My dad becomes agitated. "My daughter thinks I'm losing my mind."

"It's normal to forget things and get confused at our age," the doctor assures him. "Nobody thinks you're crazy."

I avert my eyes away from my father's glare.

The doctor looks between us, noticing the tension. "Grace, why don't you wait outside while I talk to your dad?"

I hesitate.

He opens the door, and I reluctantly get to my feet. There is so much I want to tell the doctor, but not in front of my dad. He closes the door as I step into the hallway. I pause and stare at the closed door, feeling sad, before making my way out to the waiting area. I check my emails on my phone and text Sara to make sure everything is under control at the shop. I hear the sound of creaky door hinges, and I look up to find the doctor standing there. "Grace, can I talk to you for a moment?"

I tuck my phone in my pocket and walk towards the nurse's station. He puts the clipboard down and turns to face me. "I left him in the room so we can have a quick talk."

"Is everything okay?"

"Yes. Perfect, to be honest."

I lower my brow. "I'm confused. He's definitely not okay."

He sighs. "I know. We see it all the time. Loved ones tell us patients are struggling, but when we put them through the tests for memory, function and independence, they pass with flying colours."

"He's going on garden dates with his dead wife." I remind him.

"I know. When I ask him, he's aware she's passed and knows it's impossible for her to meet him in the garden. There's no real proof of cognitive impairment or anything other than him suffering from normal occurrences of old age."

"So, what do I do? I'm terrified to leave him alone anymore."

"All we can do is keep an eye on him." He hands me a flyer from the community assistance program. "If I were you, I'd get him on a waiting list for assisted living. There is a several-year waiting list. If things get worse, please call and make an appointment."

I nod, feeling very overwhelmed.

"You can take him home now."

I open the exam room door and force myself to smile. "Are you ready to go home? The doctor says you passed with flying colours."

He grunts as he gets to his feet and shuffles past me.

We're almost halfway home when I can't take the silent treatment any longer. "Are you still mad at me?"

"I'm not mad."

I try not to smile. "Really? You look mad."

"I was mad at first. I haven't lost all my marbles, but I admit there may be a hole in the bag."

I laugh. "I just want to make sure we're doing everything we can be doing for you. I know it can't be easy."

"It's not."

I place my hand on top of his as we pull into the driveway. "I know, Dad. It's not easy for me either."

The children next door are outside playing. The sound of laughter is a welcome boost to my spirits.

"I'm going to sit in the garden," my dad announces as he exits the car.

"Okay, I'll come get you when lunch is ready." I dial Sara's number on my way into the house. She answers on the second ring. "Can you talk?"

"Yes, there's no one in the store now."

"Did you think about it?"

"I did. If you want to open to the public on the weekends, I'm willing to try it."

"That's fabulous! When?"

"Might as well start this weekend. I'm free during the day. You?"

"Yes, I'm good."

"Have you thought more about calling my nephew's friend?"

"Umm. No. I've got my hands full with my father right now."

"Just thought I'd check."

"You're persistent, I'll give you that."

"Seriously, he's a great guy. And I think you deserve to have someone in your life."

"Thank you, Sara. Now is just not the right time."

"Okay. I'll let it go…for now."

I roll my eyes. "I have to go. If we're opening on Saturday, there are some things I need to do."

"Okay. This is just a trial, right? We need for it to be busy enough on the weekends to hire a part-time student. I can't work seven days a week."

"Yes, that's the plan. I don't want to work every weekend either. The revenue generated needs to make sense."

"I'll leave the business numbers to you. Someone has just come in."

"Go sell things. I'll talk to you later."

I immediately order some smaller decorative items and farmhouse décor from the local artisans I met at the market, then use social media to spread the word.

Curiosity gets the best of me, and I search Sawyer's name to see if I can find a way to connect with him. I need a dose of his magic friendship mojo right now, but I can't seem to find him on any platforms. The door opens, and my dad steps into the room.

"I'm going to lie down, Grace. Our outing today has made me very tired."

"What about lunch? Don't you want to eat first?"

"No. I'm not hungry. I'll have a snack later when I watch my game shows."

"Okay. Let me know if you need anything."

"You'll be the first to know."

I ignore his mood swing. After all, it's been a difficult day.

I give up on stalking Sawyer and turn on the television. It doesn't look like he's much of a social media guy. It's not until I sit back down on the sofa that I notice the picture on the wall next to the window is hanging upside down. I cautiously look around as I make my way across the room and put it back the right way. I convince myself that my dad is responsible for all the bizarre things happening.

It's been a challenging week. Despite looking for him daily in town, I haven't bumped into Sawyer. Today is the first Saturday we've opened to the public. The walk-in traffic is sometimes overwhelming, but I won't know if it was a success until I crunch the numbers on Monday.

"I want to thank you for having my back this week," I say to Sara when there's a break in the crowd.

"Of course. You'd do it for me. How is your dad doing now?"

"He seems perfectly fine some days. Then he has days that worry me."

She straightens one of the displays. "That's tough."

"It is. He can still do things for himself independently. The doctor says all things are within the normal range for his age. I definitely think he's struggling with episodes of dementia or depression." I pause, feeling emotionally exhausted.

Sara hugs me and holds me tightly until I'm more worried about getting air than breaking into tears. The sadness on her face makes the pain inside me grow heavier.

She still has a firm grip on my elbows when she releases me. "We're having a barbecue tonight. I sent you an email invitation weeks ago, but you didn't R.S.V.P. Not that I'm surprised. I think you need to come."

"I don't think so, but thank you."

She holds up her hand, stopping me. "You need a day away from that house. I'm not taking no for an answer. Bring your dad if you're worried about leaving him alone." She locks the front doors.

I'm bone tired and not really in the mood for socializing.

"I'll see you later," Sara says as she grabs her purse. "Don't worry about bringing anything. I have enough food to feed a small army."

Chapter Four

Sara's not wrong. I think about it all the way home and conclude that my mother wouldn't want me to stop living any more than she'd like that for my dad. I freshen up and change my clothes at least three times before I finally settle on a cute and casual sundress. I walk out to the garden to find my dad.

He smiles as I approach. "You look very pretty."

"Thank you. I'm going to Sara's for a visit. Would you like to come with me?"

"That's kind of you to invite me." He gets to his feet and walks toward the house. "I was just about to go in and have a rest."

"Are you feeling okay? I can stay home if you're not well."

"I'm fine, Grace. I'm tired these days. I'm old, you know."

"My phone number is on the fridge. I'll go back in and take out something for you to warm up for supper. I'll leave it on the counter beside the microwave. Call me if you need anything."

"I think I can remember how to turn on the T.V."

I smile, feeling more comfortable with my decision to go out. Today is a good day. "I won't be gone long. Are you sure there's nothing you need before I go?"

"Nothing at all. Go! Have a great time."

I sit in my car in the driveway, trying to talk myself out of it. Dad was in good spirits and sounding more like himself. There's no reason not to go. A hummingbird skirts across the hood of my car and hovers at the window. I know it's looking at its reflection in the glass, but I swear it's looking right at me. When it wisps away at lightning speed, I put the car into gear and leave.

It's been so long since I've been to a social event that I overthink everything on the way over in the car. By the time I get there, I'm feeling very overwhelmed. I only recognize a few people as I walk through the backyard, searching for Sara. I'm met with smiles and a few cheerful greetings. When I run out of places to look, I stop and stand awkwardly by myself. A friendly woman with long flowing hair joins me.

"Hi, I'm Maya."

"I'm Grace."

"Oh, from the store."

"Yes."

"Sara is in the kitchen getting a few things ready. I'm going to help if you want to come with me."

"Thank you. I feel silly standing here when I don't know anyone."

"Well, it is Dufferin County. You might have arrived a stranger, but you'll have many new friends by the time you leave."

The screen door makes a loud sound as it snaps shut behind us.

"Reinforcements have arrived," Maya calls out as we approach the kitchen.

Sara's face lights up when she sees us. "Thank goodness. I don't know why I say yes to these barbecues."

Maya picks up a knife and continues slicing the tomatoes on the cutting board. "Because your husband loves to entertain, and you can't say no to him."

Sara rolls her eyes. "You're right about that part. Grace, I'm so glad that you're here. How's your dad? He didn't come?"

I manage a small smile. "He said it was kind to invite him, but he was going to have a rest and then watch his game shows."

"Is he still hallucinating?"

Maya looks up and pauses. "Hallucinating?"

I sigh. "He says he sees my mother in the garden. She's been dead a few years now."

Maya gives me a sympathetic look. "I'm sorry. It's tough watching them start to fail."

"Okay," Sara says cheerfully, tossing a bag of pretzels at me. "This is a party. No more sad talk."

Sara and I place the snacks and condiments on the table under the canopy. She grins from ear to ear. "It's your lucky day."

I turn my attention to her. "What?"

She nods in the direction of the gate. "Our nephews, Jake and his brother Ben."

My eyes open wide. "Wait, Jake McCarthy is your nephew? Why didn't you tell me?"

"I thought you might think I was giving him preferential treatment, and I wanted you to buy his stuff based on his talent and nothing else."

As they move further into the yard, a familiar face follows them.

"And *that* is Jake's friend Sawyer, whom I've been telling you about."

Our eyes meet across the yard, and Sawyer's face brightens with a wide smile. He lifts his hand to wave at me as he walks across the yard. Sara raises a brow. "Do you know each other?"

"Sawyer and I grew up together. He used to live next door."

"Well, then, you don't need me to stick around and introduce you." She walks toward the house, stopping when Sawyer intercepts her.

"Thank you again for inviting me today." He looks past her to see if I'm still there.

"You're always welcome here, Sawyer." She glances over her shoulder at me and grins before disappearing into the house.

He walks straight to me. "I'm so happy to run into you again. It seems like we keep forgetting to exchange contact information."

"So, you're the nephew's friend who's a good catch."

Sawyer laughs. "Is that what she said? That is a huge exaggeration."

"How many girls has she tried to set you up with?"

He lowers his brow. "None that I know of. Why?"

"I've been getting the hard sell."

His eyes glisten in the afternoon sun. "And are you ready to buy?"

Is he flirting with me? I hesitate, and he gives me a charming smile. A hummingbird wisps past us and hovers momentarily over a feeder at the back of the yard.

Sawyer watches it. "It's a sign, you know. The hummingbird."

I pull my summer sweater around me, attempting to conceal my shoulder tattoo. "I'm aware."

Intrigued, he lowers his brow and twists the lid off a pop bottle. "What?" he asks, noticing my amused smile. "You look like you're up to something."

"It's been a long time since we've hung out together."

"You still have the sweetest smile. I thought about you all the time."

"Really?" I raise my brow.

He looks wounded. "You don't believe me?"

"Several years have come and gone without a phone call, so..."

"I thought about it. Often. I figured you were living your best adult life, and I..."

A bearded mountain of muscle approaches us. "I'm Ben. I don't believe we've met."

I take his outstretched hand. "I'm Grace."

"THE Grace?" he pauses, looking surprised. Raising a brow, he glances at Sawyer.

Sawyer gives him a look that's a clear warning. I'm not entirely sure what's going on but I speak up. "The one and only, Grace. I didn't know I was a celebrity."

Jake joins us. He's a clean-shaven man whose muscle mass is nowhere near that of his brother's, but he's still solid and masculine. "There's a celebrity here?" he asks curiously.

"This is Grace," Ben says, gauging his reaction.

"I know Grace," he says, narrowing his eyes, confused.

"This is THE Grace," Ben says, making strange gestures with his face.

"Is he okay?" I whisper to Sawyer.

"Ignore him."

Jake pauses. "Oh, *Sawyer's* Grace. I'm sorry, I never made the connection."

I squint. "Well, why would you?"

Sawyer squirms uncomfortably. "Hey, I have an idea. Why don't you two go away."

"No one has ever accused you of being subtle," Ben laughs. He puts his hand on his brother's shoulder and steers him across the yard.

Sawyer scratches his head. "Well, that was awkward."

"I thought he was having a stroke or something. Did they grow up here?"

"They did."

"I don't remember them."

"Either did I when we became reacquainted after college. Ben has school pictures with him and me in the same elementary school classes."

I take a long, appreciative look from the other side of the yard. "You'd think every girl in town would remember him."

Sawyer quirks a brow. "I assure you he didn't look like that in grade two."

Dusk creeps in, darkening the horizon. I feel the dampness of the night's air on my skin, making me shiver.

"You're cold." He takes his hoodie off and wraps it over my shoulders. "Let's grab a seat by the fire."

With his hand firmly on my back, he guides me to the edge of a small backyard firepit. "Better?"

"Yes, thank you." I watch the flames dance around the edges of the raised brick.

"It's not the same as some of the fires we attended."

I grin. "No, it's not." Childhood memories come flooding back to me. "Do you remember the fires we had in the field at Wilson's farm?"

"Who could forget? Curtis Wilson and his brothers would get that fire blazing higher than a three-story building."

"It was a magnificent sight."

"It was. He would teepee full wooden skids and douse them with kerosene from an old copper coffee pot kept specifically for that purpose. We had no idea how dangerous that was back then."

"Nor did we care," I add. I lose his attention as he stares into the flames.

"Knowing what I know now and seeing the aftermath, I have a new respect for fire...and life."

"I bet. We didn't think about it much back then." I pick up a campfire stick and force a wiener onto the end. "That fire burned so hot you couldn't get close enough to roast anything."

"Once, my marshmallow burst into flames when I got a foot away."

I smile. "Thank goodness you didn't get any closer. You'd have no eyebrows left."

"Right? I look ridiculous without eyebrows. I know this because I singed them in a training exercise many years ago." He takes the stick out of my hand. "Here, let me do that for you." He stands at a distance with the skewer strategically placed. "So, I can't help wondering about something. I understand why you stayed in town, but why the career change?"

"I took a few intern positions out of college. It didn't take me long to realize that I hated business."

"That bad?"

"I was miserable."

"But aren't you still technically running a business now?"

"Technically. Sara and I are co-owners, so we share the operating functions."

"How did you meet?"

"A friend of mine knows her. When she found out Sara was looking for a business partner, she introduced us. At first, I wasn't sure about being in the business of up-cycling or design. But it fascinated me. Every item has a story and a history."

"Sounds like you found your calling." Sawyer hands me back the stick. "Not black, but not cold."

I reach for it, admiring his skill. "The perfect campfire dog." Something passes between us as our eyes lock over a smouldering hot dog on a metal skewer. Sawyer quirks a smile, and I suddenly feel giddy and nervous simultaneously. Growing up, he was my best friend, and I don't know why I suddenly feel self-conscious about eating a wiener while he watches. Sawyer says nothing. He stares straight at me with a silly, boyish grin.

I'm shocked when I glance at the time on my phone and see it's after midnight. "I have to get going," I say, feeling panicked.

"So soon? I'm sorry. Did I say something wrong? Was it the eyebrows? Or the wiener?"

"No," I laugh. "Nothing like that. I didn't realize it was so late. I should get home. My dad hasn't been himself these days, and I probably shouldn't have left him alone this long."

"I'll walk you to your car."

I search every pocket, and possible place my keys could reside as we walk.

"What's wrong?"

"I can't find my keys."

"Did you put them down somewhere?"

"No, I don't think so. I remember I had them when…." I raise my brow and walk over to the driver's side window. I lean forward and strain my neck, looking inside. I grit my teeth and curse.

"You locked them in the car?"

"I did." My shoulders drop, feeling defeated.

"Do you have a spare key?"

I shake my head.

Sawyer laughs. "It's late. Why don't I drive you home? I have a friend who works for a towing company and has the tools to open the door. I'll call him in the morning and look after it, unless you need your car tonight."

I considered it for a moment but couldn't think of any reasonable reason why I would. "I don't want to be any trouble."

"It's no trouble at all." He places his hand on my back and guides me down the street, switching sides to ensure I walk furthest away from any potential traffic. It's a heroic gesture Sawyer practiced even when we were kids.

We drive the several blocks in just a few minutes. I'm intrigued when Sawyer parks and then gets out of the truck. I pull the handle to open the door, and he rushes to hold it open while I get out.

"What are you doing?"

"I just want to see you get to the door safely."

I look around me at the quiet street.

"You never know who could be hiding in the bushes," he says defensively.

Right on queue, the bushes rustle, causing us both to become nervous. I move closer to Sawyer until my body is pressed against his. He takes a protective stance. A large momma skunk emerges, followed by several babies.

"How are you going to protect me against her?" I laugh.

"I'd throw myself in front of you if she attacked."

I quirk a brow. "And if she sprays?"

"It's a stinky chance I'd take to ensure m'lady is safe."

That is classic Sawyer, always heroic and genuine. Maybe he played a few too many games of Dungeons and Dragons, but I'm relieved that adulting hasn't discouraged all those traits. The world can be cruel. The momma skunk watches her babies cross the street and then follows. "I think we're safe now," I whisper.

"Wow, our old house doesn't look any different." He notes as he walks me to the door.

"It hasn't changed much on the outside, but they completely gutted the inside."

"From what I remember, I can't say I blame them."

"Thank you for bringing me home." I can't seem to stop smiling. "It was nice catching up."

"Are your house keys on the same ring as your car?"

I throw my head back. "Ugh. Yes, locked in my car."

He walks to the garden's edge and rolls back the fake stone that houses the spare key. Pleased with himself, he holds it in the air and returns to the door. I try to take it from him, but he holds on tight, not letting go. I look at him curiously.

"You need to find a more secure spot for that," he says as he releases it.

I frown. "I know, but it's been in the same place for thirty years. Lately, Dad has become so confused I don't want to start changing things on him."

"It's a good idea to leave it then. You're a great daughter, Grace."

"I tried putting in a security system after mom passed because I kept finding the doors wide open, and some creepy shit was happening. He couldn't grasp it and set it off several times a day. The security company finally told me they would stop responding to calls."

"My parents struggle with today's technology. I know how hard it is for your dad."

"It's been a struggle lately." I pause. "I've been out of the house most of the day, so I should go in and check on him."

"You probably should."

There's an awkward silence, and I'm unsure why I'm still standing there.

"Can I have your phone?"

"What?" I ask, confused.

"Your phone. I'll put my number in your contacts."

I pass it to him. "Oh, of course."

He quickly adds his number and passes it back to me. "Goodnight, Grace."

In the muted lighting of the front porch, I feel like I'm back in high school.

"Do you remember that night you walked me home from the house party after someone called the police?"

He chuckles. "I do. We stood here trying to unlock the door without waking your parents."

"But my mother was standing on the other side of the door and started flashing the lights on and off, thinking we were making out."

"I remember."

"Crazy that she thought you'd be out here kissing me."

Sawyer says nothing but holds my gaze. Right on queue, the light flickers. Sawyer looks up at it, then raises a brow. "Tell me that's a coincidence, or there's a short in the wiring."

"I told you." I raise my shoulders. "Creepy shit." I unlock the door and turn to get one more glimpse of his smile. "Good night." I close the door behind me and take a deep breath before peeking out the window to watch him walk back to his truck. Every time he walked me home I watched him cross the yard toward his house. He pauses before opening the truck door and looks back at the house as if he knows I'm watching.

"What are you looking at?"

Startled, I gasp and spin around. "Dad!" I let out a sigh of relief. "You scared the crap out of me. What are you doing sitting in the dark?"

"I suppose I just fell asleep here."

I make my way across the room and help him to his feet. "Do you need help?"

"No, I'm fine," he says as he shuffles across the carpet to the main floor bedroom.

When he closes the door, there's a strange creaking on the steps, and I catch a glimpse of a shadow. I turn on all the lights to confirm that no one is there and quickly climb the stairs before rushing to my room. I flop on the bed, too tired to get undressed. "Some days, I feel like I'm living in a Stephen King novel."

Chapter Five

I wake in the morning feeling like I had a great night's sleep. I must have been so exhausted that I didn't even dream. If I did, I don't remember what it was about.

My dad is sitting at the kitchen table, eating a bowl of cereal. I'm relieved that it looks like it will be a good day for him. My shoulders fall as I look at the counter. "You didn't eat the dinner I left for you?"

"Dinner?"

"Yes, the plate I left you on the counter. Did you eat anything after I went out yesterday?"

He becomes flustered. "I don't remember. I must have."

I dump the dinner contents into the compost bin under the sink. "I've forgotten many things in my day, but I've never forgotten to eat," I tease, trying to lighten the moment and ease his frustration. I lean against the counter and search for local towing companies to unlock my car doors. "Will you be okay for a few minutes? I have to walk over to Sara's and get my car."

"I'll be fine."

I give the person on the other end all my information, and they place me on hold to confirm.

"Hello?"

"Yes, I'm here."

"It seems we've already unlocked your vehicle, and it's coming to you."

I'm confused. "It's on the way to me?"

"Yes, ma'am. It should be there in a moment."

There's that word again. "It's being towed?" I walk to the window and look up the street.

"It doesn't say that we're towing. It just says it's on route."

My car appears from one of the connecting streets, and I wrinkle a brow.

"I see it now. Thank you very much." I hang up the phone and open the front door. I let out a single laugh and shake my head when Sawyer pulls into the driveway and honks.

"I was just on the phone with the towing company."

He gets out of the car and laughs. "I told you I had a friend who could take care of it."

"I suppose I'm lucky that's the company I called."

"Not so lucky. I think they're the only service in town."

"How are you getting home?"

"Jake and Ben are at Sara's. Jake's been itching to get his hands on my new truck, so he's driving it over, and Ben will follow him."

"They seem like good people."

"Jake and Ben? I wish more people held themselves to their standard. They both have their own businesses, help their aging father with his, and on the weekends, they help all

50

their neighbours with haying and whatever other farm chores need to be done.”

“That’s incredible.”

“They make me feel like an underachiever.”

“You’re kidding, right?” I don’t know anybody more selfless than Sawyer.

Sawyer rolls his eyes as Jake comes squealing around the corner in his pickup and screeches to a stop in the driveway. Jake chuckles as he climbs down out of the cab.

“Really?” Sawyer responds, unimpressed, with his arms crossed.

“What’s the point of having all that power if you’re not going to *drive* it?”

“I get your point, but it’s not the getaway vehicle from a bank heist.”

Arriving a few moments later, Ben parks and walks up the driveway. He clips his brother in the back of the head as he joins us. “What’s the matter with you? Kids are playing on this street.”

Sawyer laughs. “Thanks, guys. I appreciate it.”

Jake rubs the back of his head and gives his brother an annoyed look. “No worries, we had to drop some stuff off to Aunt Sara anyway. What are your plans for the rest of the day?”

“I’m heading up to visit Curtis Wilson. Sitting around that fire last night brought back some old memories, so I messaged him this morning. He’s living up in Grey County now.” He turns to me and grins. “You should come with me!”

“Oh, I don’t think so.”

"Why not? Do you have plans?"

"Well, no, but I still feel guilty about leaving my dad alone yesterday."

"Hey," Jake interrupts. "Doesn't he know our father from the men's group at church? Why don't we take him out to the farm for a visit?"

"I'm not even sure he'll remember your dad. He hasn't gone to the men's fellowship in a long time."

"We could ask. We've got things to do around the property today, and Dad insists on helping, and quite frankly, we'd rather he had company and stayed out of the way."

Sawyer looks at me with pleading eyes. "It's a beautiful day for a drive through the country."

I shrug. "Okay, let's go ask him." I'm confident he'll say no.

The boys follow me into the backyard. Sawyer lets out an audible expression of appreciation. "I'd forgotten how beautiful this garden is."

I smile. "My mom and dad made sure they created an oasis in the middle of the suburbs."

"You wouldn't even know there are houses around them," Ben adds.

"I know. It's so peaceful back here. It's where he spends all his time now." We find him sitting in his favourite spot on the cement bench. "Hey, Dad! We have visitors."

My heart sinks a little when he turns with a stoic look and pauses. It wasn't that long ago he thought Sawyer and his parents still lived next door. A slow smile curls across his lips, and his eyes light up. I'm dumbfounded when he gets to his feet, seemingly excited.

"Sawyer!" he says with enthusiasm.

Sawyer smiles and extends his hand. "Nice to see you again, sir."

My dad pulls him into a firm hug, wrapping his arms around him and patting him on the back. "It's been too long. I heard you were in Alberta."

"Yes, I worked with the Ministry of Forestry out there. I mostly dealt with conservation management and forest fire prevention."

"That's wonderful!" he says delighted. "Wait." He looks past Sawyer at Ben and Jake. "You're Phillip McCarthy's boys, right?"

They grin as they shake his hand. "Yes, sir. It's nice to see you again."

"So many visitors in one day." He says, looking more excited than I've seen in a long time. "What are you doing here?"

"We were in town and had to stop to pick up Sawyer. We got talking, and we're wondering if you would like to come with us out to the farm to visit with our dad for a few hours while Sawyer and Grace run a few errands. Dad would love to see you."

"Today?"

Ben's smile softens his mountainous appearance. "Yes, sir. We're heading out there right now."

I wait while he pauses and thinks about it. I prepare myself for his refusal. He doesn't want to go anywhere these days.

"I'd like that."

"But?" I ask, waiting for the other shoe to drop.

"But I'd like to be home in time to watch my game shows before supper."

Jake nods. "Absolutely. I promise to have you home by then."

"I'll get you a jacket and a hat and meet you out front." I rush into the house, afraid he'll change his mind. I grab my purse and his stuff from the chair in the front hall and lock the front door behind me. The guys already have him situated in the front seat of Ben's truck by the time I get outside. He looks so excited and full of life right now. My heart feels overjoyed. Jake takes his hat and jacket out of my hands and gets in the back seat.

"Thank you."

Jake smiles and leans out the open window. "Oh, don't you worry. One day, we may be dropping our father off here for the day."

I laugh. "Anytime."

Sawyer puts his arm on my back and gently rubs it in a caring way. "Message or call if there are any problems," he says as Ben drives away. He turns to me with a wide grin. "Are you ready?"

I look at him suspiciously. "Why are you so happy?"

"Because it's been a long time since I spent the day with my best friend. I missed her." He holds the door and helps me into the oversized cab of his truck. "Hope you don't mind the backroads," he says as he jumps into the driver's seat.

"Not at all. I haven't been out for a drive in a very long time. Probably the last time was with you."

"What? You're kidding me?"

"No. I'm not."

"Where did we go?" He scratches his head, trying to recall.

"We were supposed to be going to a party somewhere in Dundalk, but we ended up somewhere on a beach in Grand Bend."

"I remember now." He avoids looking at me, but I can see his mischievous grin.

"I always thought it was odd that you got lost that night. You always knew your way around."

He rubs his neck and glances at me quickly. "Well, it's been a long time, so I guess I can tell you now."

"Tell me what?"

"That wasn't an accident."

"What wasn't?"

Sawyer turns quickly onto a gravel sideroad, and I have to hold the handle to keep from bouncing around.

"Getting lost. I knew where the party was. I didn't want to go."

I squint my eyes. "Why didn't you just say so?"

He shrugs. "I thought you wanted to go."

"Pfft. No. I hate being around people. Drunk people are even worse."

"I didn't know that. I feel the same way, but I didn't want you to be upset with me."

"I wasn't disappointed at all. That was such a beautiful night. The sky was clear, and the moon reflected off the water."

"There was a sparkle in your eyes that night that I'll never forget."

I get a weird flutter inside me, and I look away, trying to avoid his eyes and awkward feelings. We ride silently for a few kilometres up the road until he pulls into the gas station for fuel. "Do me a favour?" He peels a couple of twenty-dollar bills out of a wad of cash in his pocket.

"Sure?" Anything to break this weird silence.

"I feel like we should grab some beverages and snacks to take with us."

"It would be rude to show up empty-handed."

"It would. Then we're also prepared in case we get lost."

My head snaps to the side to look at him. He laughs, and I realize he's teasing me.

When I return to the truck with a bag of snacks, he's still pumping fuel. I cringe as I see the total on the pump.

"I know, it's shocking." He hangs up the nozzle and opens the driver's side door.

"Can I ask you a question?" I ask as he pulls back onto the road.

"Sure."

I lean forward and turn the radio down. "I thought you were taking Police Sciences in college?"

"That's where I started. I attended several career fairs and discovered that conservation officers required police training, but there was a side of forestry that intrigued me, so I jumped on board."

"Well, that suits you more than being a cop."

"You think so?"

"Definitely. I knew you were destined to save the world, but I could never imagine you making drug busts and sitting behind the town population sign waiting to catch speeders."

He smiles. "Once I started down that road, I quickly realized it wasn't for me."

"Looks like we both changed gears for the better."

"I think so."

His phone rings, and he answers the call on Bluetooth. "Hey, Curtis."

"Hey, Sawyer. I'm so sorry, but I have to cancel today. Something came up."

I feel disappointed.

"No worries. It happens."

"I hope you aren't on your way already."

"We are."

"We?"

"I kidnapped Grace. She was coming with me."

"Now I feel like a knucklehead. Tell her I'm so sorry."

"You're on speaker, brother. She can hear you."

"I'm sorry, Grace. I'm working on this huge charity event, and it's a real shit show right now."

"It's okay, Curt. Is there something that Sawyer and I can help with?"

"That's kind of you, but not today. I might reach out later if I don't lose my mind."

"Let us know if there's anything we can do."

"Thanks, man. Sorry again."

Sawyer disconnects the call and frowns. "Well, we're not heading in the right direction to head to Grand Bend, but we could keep driving and find somewhere to have lunch in one of the small towns on Georgian Bay. Maybe drive around Collingwood and see what's going on?"

It is a beautiful day, and wasting it would be a shame. I suddenly feel apprehensive. "Can we check on my dad first?"

"Of course we can. I'm sure he's doing fine." He pulls over at one of the many gorgeous lookout spots and parks his truck. Jake answers on the first ring.

"How's everything going?"

"Great, how's your visit?"

"Curt cancelled, so we were thinking about going for a little drive and maybe stopping for lunch. Are you guys good for a couple of hours? How is Stan?"

"He's great! They've been chattering non-stop."

"That's great, but I need proof of life."

"Will do. Be safe and have fun. We've got this."

"Thanks, buddy. Call if anything changes."

"Proof of life?" I ask curiously as he hangs up. He grins as his text notification pings a few times. He opens the message and hands me his phone. I scroll through several pictures of my dad sitting and enjoying a beverage with Mr.

McCarthy and several pictures of them laughing and having what seems to be a great time.

"Oh, I get it now." I laugh, feeling silly.

"Feel better?"

"I do."

"Great. Should we do some research before we get on the road again or drive toward the bay and see where we land?"

"Let's drive and see where we end up."

Sawyer grins. "That's my girl. Still brave and adventurous."

I lower my brow. "I wouldn't say I was an adventurous child."

We pull back onto the main road and head towards the Georgian Bay area. "You were always up for anything, as I remember."

I laugh. "Only because I knew I'd be safe and have a good time as long as I was with you."

"The same holds true today."

"That's a relief."

I gasp when one of our favourite classic rock songs comes on the radio. Sawyer glances at me when I lean forward and turn up the volume. This is what I have been missing—these moments of pure happiness. I roll down the window and put my feet on the dash. Sawyer keeps looking over at my shoes, likely worried about footprints on the interior dash of his truck, but he doesn't say a word. He just sings along with me while he drives.

Chapter Six

We slowly drive the main street of the first small town on our journey. "Look, there's a spot opening up on the street just ahead."

Sawyer pulls in and parks. "The Rusty Nail. Does this place look okay to you?"

"Sure. If we can get a seat. It looks pretty crowded."

Sawyer opens my door and holds out his hand. I slide out of the truck like a small child at the playground. "Why do they have to make them so high?" I complain.

He grins. "I guess it's a good sign it's busy. The food must be good." He opens the door for me and then follows me in.

"Grab a seat anywhere," a voice yells from somewhere unknown.

I shrug and enter the dining area. There's a spot for two by the window, so I make my way in that direction. "Is this okay?" I ask him as we reach it.

"Of course." He pulls out the chair for me and waits until I'm seated.

"You haven't changed at all," I note aloud.

He sits across from me and cocks his head to the side. "Is that a good thing or a bad thing?"

"Definitely good. Most guys stop doing kind things after a while."

"I suppose most people, not just guys, stop doing as many kind or thoughtful things as they get comfortable in a relationship."

"Fair point." I pick up my menu and raise my brow. "There are way too many choices."

"Narrow it down. What are you not in the mood for?"

"Salad."

"What kind of twisted person orders a salad at a bar?" He tries to hide an amused look. "Sandwich? Burger?"

"I'm thinking wings."

He folds his menu and places it in front of him. "Done. Me too."

He orders a couple of beers and a few pounds of wings. I'm not surprised that he remembers how we used to order them when we were in high school. And unlike back then, Sawyer devoured four wings for every one I ate.

"Can I ask you something now?" he asks, licking the sauce off his fingers.

"I suppose."

"That day, at the market. Did you see me?"

"What? No!"

"Oh, okay. I thought when I was looking around that I saw you and that you saw me. I was trying to figure out why you pretended not to."

My face turns red. "I thought I heard your voice. But I couldn't see you. I thought I was imagining things."

He nods, swallows the last mouthful of beer, and signals to the waitress for the bill.

"Why did you come back after all this time?"

"Well. It wasn't the plan originally. My aunt passed away and left me the sole heir of her estate. I had planned on coming home and selling everything, but then I got here and saw the property."

"You couldn't pass it up?"

"Oh, hell no. I was terrified. It's a disaster."

I laugh. "Really?"

"Don't get me wrong; it's huge and stunning, but it's run-down, and needs a lot of work."

"So, why are you staying?"

"Once I got here, I realized I've been homesick for a long time and didn't know it. This is where I belong."

I can't say I'm disappointed. Sawyer waves me off when I take out my wallet. "I've got this."

I get to my feet and walk toward the door. "I'll get it next time."

"We'll see."

When he stands to walk toward me, my eyes lock on his tall, muscular body and broad shoulders. His wide smile makes my heart beat with a cadence I wasn't expecting.

He looks at the time on his phone. "We have time to walk down to the water."

"I'm in."

I'm acutely aware of how close he is as we walk toward the waterfront. Our hands brush together, and I resist tangling our fingers together. It seems like a natural thing to do, but I have no idea what would happen if I did.

The onshore breeze is cool and a welcoming contrast from the midday heat. The sun reflects brightly off the water, making his brown eyes glisten like the colour of dark whiskey. They are just as potent as his smile. I don't recall ever noticing that before. He catches me staring, and I quickly avert my gaze.

It must be the sun and fresh air that's making me behave so strangely today.

"This isn't a sandy beach, but we can walk along the rocks if you like?"

I slip off my shoe and dip my toe into the water. "Not a chance."

"I don't blame you. We can walk back through town."

It sounded like a good idea until I realized that the walk back to the truck was uphill all the way. Sawyer extends his elbow for me to hold on to as a lifeline. If I wasn't before, I'm now acutely aware of the size of his biceps. He stops in front of a brightly painted shop halfway through town. "Ice cream!"

I struggle to catch my breath. "It says it's the best ice cream in town."

"How can we walk by?"

"Let me guess. You want ice cream?"

"When was the last time you stopped for ice cream?"

I pause. Dare I tell him that, too, was with him?

"We're getting ice cream," he declares without waiting for my answer. He practically drags me inside. The number of handwritten flavours written on a blackboard is intimidating. It takes me several minutes before I settle on rum and raisin.

"I'll have vanilla," Sawyer announces to the girl behind the counter.

My eyes open wide. "vanilla?"

He nods.

"What happened to the guy who once engaged in an hour-long debate on how chocolate was the best ice cream flavour in the entire universe?"

He chuckles and shrugs. "Nothing beats a really good vanilla."

I scowl. "I don't even know how we're still friends."

"I'm pretty sure we did a blood pact."

"Absolutely not."

"Spit handshake?"

I cringe. "Ew. I would never."

He pushes open the door and exits onto the street. "I'm pretty sure there was some kind of ritual we did," he says.

I lick dripping ice cream from around the cone. "Pretty sure it was a pinky swear."

"Ah. The most unbreakable of all pacts. You're stuck with me."

I glance at the incline to get to his truck. "Ugh."

"You aren't as adventurous as I remembered."

"I'm really not."

"Do you want me to get the truck and come pick you up?"

I consider it a minute, then sigh. "No. I can do this."

He offers his hand, and I willingly accept it. Not too much farther along the way, I feel an aching pain in my heel. "What's going on?" he asks, noticing my limp.

"I think I've got a blister."

"Not surprised. Who wears sneakers without socks?"

"Probably most of the population, thank you," I say, annoyed. "I was wearing slippers when you arrived. When Dad said he'd go, I was so worried that if I ran upstairs to get socks, he'd change his mind."

"Well, then. There's only one solution." He sweeps me up into his arms, holding me beneath my knees.

"Put me down this minute!" I insist. "I'm not an invalid."

"How about over my shoulder like a damsel in distress?"

"NO!"

He sets me down and steadies me until both feet are planted firmly on the ground. "Okay, there's only one solution, and I'm not taking no for an answer." He stands in front of me and bends over.

"What are you doing?"

He glances over his shoulder. "Climb on."

"A piggyback?"

"Yes, now climb on."

"I'm too heavy," I protest.

"Nonsense. It's not that far up the hill. I have to be able to carry victims out of the woods to safety. It's my job."

I know I'm going to regret this. I position myself behind him and place my hands on his back.

"Whenever you're ready, hop up and wrap your arms and legs around me."

Here goes nothing. I do as he says, and he firmly grasps my legs as they wrap around him. I squeal as he stands upright and begins to walk the incline. "This is bizarre," I complain.

"I can put you down and go get the truck."

"No, we're almost there. I'll tough it out."

"*YOU'LL* tough it out?" he says, grunting.

People stare at us as they pass. The few blocks back to the restaurant seem like a hundred miles away. Finally, he slides me to the ground beside his truck. "We made it, m'lady," he says, bowing majestically. He opens the door and lifts me into the seat.

"What are you doing?" I ask as he reaches down and pulls off my shoes.

"I have a first aid kit in the backseat. I want to get something on that before it gets worse."

I wiggle my toes like a small child while waiting for him to administer first aid. I admit watching him fuss over something as insignificant as a blister with the utmost tenderness is sweet.

"There. All done." He gently presses the edges of the bandage to make sure it sticks. "I hope you like dinosaurs. I couldn't find any adult ones."

"I'm good with dinosaurs."

"No more shoes with no socks."

"Yes, sir!" I mock.

He gets in the car and sends Jake a message to tell him we're on our way home. The music and the laughter continue the entire drive back to Dufferin County. When he pulls into the driveway, I realize I don't want this day to end.

Jake arrives at the perfect time and we watch as he helps my dad to the house.

"He's got to be exhausted. I can't remember the last time he went out anywhere."

"Thanks, Jake," I say as they approach.

"No problem. My dad had a fantastic time as well. They spent hours talking about all the men they know and what they're doing now, if they're still alive."

Dad walks past me, pulls himself up the steps, and enters the house. "I'll be in in a minute," I call to him.

"So?" Jake says with a mischievous grin.

I raise my brow. "So?"

"How was your date?"

"Date?" I look at Sawyer, confused. "It wasn't a date. Right?"

Sawyer gives Jake a warning look. "No, of course not. People who have romantic interests in each other go on dates."

"Right," I confirm. "We're just two old friends hanging out." Why do I feel disappointed when I say that aloud?

"Exactly," Sawyer confirms.

Jake looks between the two of us and smirks. "Yeah, okay. There's no romantic interest here." He walks away and stops before getting into his truck. He looks in our direction, shakes his head, and laughs before opening the door and climbing in.

"Your friends are very strange."

"Agreed."

"Grace?" my father calls from inside the house.

"Coming!"

Sawyer looks at me as if there's something he wants to say. There's an awkward pause before my dad calls my name again. "I should get going and get him sorted out."

"Of course."

He says my name as I turn away. I've never heard him speak it with such an unsettled tone. I turn back to meet his dispirited expression.

"Sawyer?" I prompt.

He sighs, and there's an awkward moment where he stumbles with his words. "I just wanted to say I had a great time today."

I smile. "Me too." I watch as he turns and walks toward his truck. Why does he look so sad if he had such a great day? He pauses and waves before climbing into his truck. I'm suddenly overcome with an unpleasant déjà vu.

Chapter Seven

"Hey!" I jump when Sara throws a roll of packaging tape at me from across the room.

"Earth to Grace." She says, amused. "You've been daydreaming all morning. What's going on with you?"

"Nothing." My blush gives it away.

"Does it have something to do with the handsome volunteer firefighter you've been spending time with?"

"No."

She gives me a look of disbelief.

"Well, maybe."

"Mmhmm."

"I love being with him again. It's like old times. Only…"

"Something is different."

"Yes! I don't know what it is."

"How long has it been since you've been in a relationship?"

"A few years. What does that have to do with anything?"

"Honey, anyone can see that he's no longer looking at you as his best friend from high school."

I'm confused. "Yesterday, there were a few moments when I had…*feelings* I wasn't expecting. But Sawyer told Jake that there was no romantic interest between us."

"Isn't there? Or did Sawyer say that because he's unsure how you feel?"

I sit silently.

"Mmhmm," she says again. She places a box of merchandise on the table in front of me and leans in. "You better open your eyes soon, or you'll miss out on something wonderful."

Sara leaves the office, and lets me ponder her advice. The sun beams through the window and warms the room, making me feel overheated. Flustered, I tug off my sweater and toss it over a stack of boxes in the corner. When I return to my desk, I catch the reflection of my tattoo in the antique mirror leaning against the wall on the other side of the room. I brush my hand over the brilliant colours and sigh.

"Hi."

I place my hand on my chest. "Sawyer! You startled me. What are you doing here?"

He holds up his first aid kit. "Checking on my patient. I thought we might need to change the dressing."

"By dressing, do you mean another dinosaur adhesive bandage?"

He holds up two boxes. "We could do dinosaurs…or…we could do kittens."

I gasp and grab the box out of his hands. "Definitely kittens!"

"Grab a seat."

I sit on the edge of my desk, and he lifts my foot. His shoulders drop, and he frowns. "Where the fuck are your socks?"

"Oh." I try to think of a quick excuse, but there's no point. He gently pries my sneaker off my foot.

"Could you at least wear slippers or sandals around the office and let it heal for a few days?"

"I could try." I shrug, feeling embarrassed.

He shakes his head, clearly frustrated. After applying a dab of antibiotic ointment, he secures another bandage over the tender, blistered skin. I hop off the desk and slip my foot back into my shoe. Sawyer turns away. "I can't even watch."

I laugh once. "You know me well enough, so you shouldn't be surprised."

"I'm starting to remember. It's nice getting reacquainted."

"It is."

Sawyer busies himself with packing away his supplies.

"So...where is the farmhouse that your aunt left you?"

"In Mono."

"Oh, so it's close by."

"Not too far out of town. But far enough."

"I'd love to see it. I've always been obsessed with century homes and their history."

"It's a little rustic, but you can stop by whenever you have time."

"She's available right now!" Sara hollers from the other room.

I roll my eyes. "Apparently, I'm available right now."

"What a coincidence. So am I, although I am on call. We'll hope for an uneventful afternoon in the community."

"I'll follow you in my car in case you get called away."

"Probably a good plan."

I pick up my things. "Sara, I'm leaving for the day!"

"Thank goodness," she yells from the hallway.

Sawyer laughs.

"Should I stay for no other reason but to annoy her?"

"No."

"No? Are you sure? I'd like to stick around to get on her nerves."

"I can hear you!" Sara says, pausing in the doorway.

"Oh," I try to hold back a smile. "I'll be leaving now." I knock over a small table, and Sawyer scrambles to grab it. "Going. Right now."

"Goodbye," Sara says with her arms crossed.

I wave as I close the door behind me. Sara has the widest smile on her face. I might be out of my mind, but I need to explore what's happening between Sawyer and me.

He's waiting in his truck, and I walk to the driver's side window and tap until he opens it. "I'll follow you. Don't lose me."

"I won't." The engine on his big V8 revs up and rumbles while it idles. I raise a brow. "If I lose you, I'll pull over on the shoulder and wait. But you have my phone number," he reminds me. "If we get separated and you lose track of me, just call."

Our town is a developing suburban city less than an hour from Toronto. Even less time to get to any of the Six. A trendy nickname used to identify the original municipalities that form the Greater Toronto Area. Well, at least that's what some people think. Others accept a famous local rapper's explanation that the Six represents the two different area codes '416' and '647'.

I follow Sawyer through the beautiful countryside of the Hills of the Headwaters, in awe that such beauty exists so close to such an overpopulated metropolis. Not even fifteen minutes away from where our journey began we're on a dirt road and heading into agricultural country. Sawyer slows his speed on the loose gravel and turns onto a long, tree-lined driveway.

I pull up behind him and get out of the car. "You wouldn't want to shovel that one by hand."

"Definitely not. I imagine back when the farm was established, they used a tractor to clear it, though I'm not entirely sure they needed to go anywhere in the middle of winter back then."

"That's true. They probably had preserved food in the cold cellar and lived off the land and their livestock."

Sawyer turns to face the more than a century-old home. "Every time I look at this place, I wonder what life would have been like back then. Sadly, right now, it's nothing but a huge house with many dusty rooms."

"How long have you been back?" I ask curiously.

"Technically, I only relocated permanently a few weeks ago. Until then, I was back and forth. There's so much to do it's overwhelming at times. And I need to focus on finding full-time employment." As he pushes his shoulder against the century-old farm door to force it open, I try not to laugh.

As I step into the front foyer, I'm teleported back in time. I can't help but smile. "A little rustic?"

"I don't know if my family were the original owners who built the house. I only know for certain that it's been owned by my family for at least a hundred years, being passed down to a few generations. I don't think any of her owners changed a thing. Jake and Ben are going to help me restore her. I want to update and freshen her up but keep her character and charm."

"When was it built?"

"From what I was told, the land was bought from the county back in the early 1800's. I haven't had time to go to the town office and look up any of the details on the house build."

"But you will?"

"I definitely will. I'm intrigued about the history."

"Seems like a good reason to stay."

He gives me a half-smile. "Partly. I'm hoping there's another reason for me to stay."

Is it me? Do I want it to be me? I'm not sure what to say. I wasn't expecting this turn of events when I wished my best friend back to town.

"Hey, I want to show you something outside. Come with me."

The grounds are overgrown from years of neglect. I follow him down a dirt pathway toward several outbuildings.

He steadies me on the muddy, uneven ground. "Where are we going?"

"Here." He pulls back branches from an overgrown bush and pulls at long grass to reveal a pale grey gravestone covered in moss and algae.

"Somebody was buried here?"

"It mentions something about it in the deed. I can't make out the words. They're too worn."

I try to blow some of the dust and dirt from the etched stone, but it does little to make things clearer. "McLaughlin. That would be my guess. I can't make out the date. Eighteen something."

"Another mystery to solve with the historical society."

"I think I remember an article recently about the history of Mono Mills. At one time, it was a bigger city than Orangeville. I think the McLaughlins were among the first Irish settlers here."

"Interesting. My family ancestry goes way back to Ireland. I don't remember any McLaughlins in the family tree. I can't wait to figure it all out."

The tall grass a few feet away starts to sway, but there's no wind. I open my eyes, concerned about what's lurking there. A very small calico cat peaks her head through the brush, gauging if it's safe.

"Hello, kitten," Sawyer says cheerfully.

"You have a cat?" I ask, surprised.

"No. She came with the house. She might be one of the neighbour's barn cats, but she always seems to be here. She's brought me a couple of dead peace offerings."

"Ew, that's disgusting."

"Well, that's not a very nice thing to say. From the size of her, I'd say she doesn't get too many meals, and she chose to share a few with me."

I frown. "Now I feel bad."

She cautiously walks toward us, and Sawyer crouches down, holding out his hand. She rubs her head along his fingertips but keeps her distance. He glances over at me and finds me watching with a look of adoration.

"I'm surprised you haven't coaxed her into the house and tried to feed her."

Sawyer scoops up the wee girl and stands. "Who says I haven't tried?" He holds her gently against his chest and rubs her ears and chin until she's purring so loudly I can hear her from a few feet away.

"What can I say?" Sawyer looks over at me. "My taste in women hasn't changed any. I have a *type*."

I want to ask him if *the girl next door* is his type. Then, it would put any question to rest. I can't deny that when he looks at me with those soulful brown eyes, my feelings seem to be shifting into something more. Do I want to risk our friendship on the chance of a failed romance? How stupid will I look if I'm misreading his signals?

He gently places the small cat back on the ground and begins to walk toward the house. I notice as we walk that the bushes in the garden are bursting with buds beginning to explode into fragrant blooms and vibrant colours.

"I bet this spot is beautiful in the summer."

"It probably was in it's day." He lifts a fallen branch off the path and tosses it to the side. The noise startles the small calico cat, and she scurries into the bush. "The goal is to get it back there again. I need to make the house liveable first. I'm not going to lie. It seems like an insurmountable task at times, and I've only just started."

"Historical restoration is Ben's profession, right? He would be a huge help."

"He would be. It's not right to ask him to do it for free. There wasn't much cash that came with the inheritance, so I need to get working as soon as possible."

"Are there a lot of jobs in your profession around here?"

He stops at the front of the house and leans against his truck. "A few. I'm open to positions that require variations of my overall skillset. I've got a few interviews lined up."

"That's really exciting."

He grins, and I notice his rugged jawline in a way I've never appreciated it before. It's strong and masculine, like his broad shoulders and heavily muscled arms.

"Grace?" he asks curiously. "You okay?"

"Yes," I answer, embarrassed that my distraction was that obvious.

"I was saying tomorrow is the movie in the park. Would you go with me?"

"Oh," I hesitate.

He reaches for my hand. "Before you answer me, I have an idea. Let's take your father with us."

"I haven't been to the movie in the park since we were kids. Dad would probably love it."

"Great!" he says, pleased. "I'll pick you up after supper. You leave all the arrangements to me. I'll look after everything." There's an awkward pause again. "Do you want to come in for tea?"

I think about it, and I really want to, but I can't. "Thanks, but I should get home. Another time?"

His eyes sparkle with hope. "Anytime you want."

I feel emotions stir inside me, and as I walk to the car, I look over my shoulder several times to find him leaning against the front porch post, watching me, with his legs crossed and an expression I can't put a name to.

Chapter Eight

I'm not sure why I spend the entire day trying to decide what to wear. I never worried about how I looked when I hung out with Sawyer before. I mull over a few super cute summer outfits, but my intuition tells me it will get cool, and there will be bugs. I decide on something casual and practical and head downstairs. My dad emerges from his room, freshly shaved and with his hair combed. He looks like the man I remember, and I feel a little choked up. I'm thrilled he willingly agreed to join us.

There's a quick knock at the door, and I hear Sawyer's voice call out. "Hello? Are you ready?"

I pull the door open all the way. "We are."

"Do you need a hand with anything?"

"Do we need chairs? Or a blanket?"

Sawyer holds up his hand. "I told you I'd look after everything."

"Famous last words. Bug Spray?"

"Errr, no. I didn't bring that."

"Hah!" I say, pleased with myself, as I grab it from the table in the front hallway.

My dad insists on sitting in the back seat. He talks about all the people who used to live on the street when he and my mom first bought their house. Now, almost everyone but him has moved on. We drive down the street toward the main entrance to the park, looking for a spot, but there's already nothing left. Sawyer drives around the block and onto a dirt path with a closed gate. A young boy wearing a reflective vest opens the barricade.

Sawyer glances at me and grins. "It's a perk of being a volunteer firefighter."

"Oh, are you working tonight?"

"Not exactly. I volunteered to be a volunteer."

I scratch my head. "Whatever that means."

"They are fully staffed, but if they need me, they'll message me."

There may have been no parking on the street, but the green space in the middle of town is vast, and there are plenty of empty spaces for us to set up chairs and enjoy the movie.

I take a drink out of Sawyer's hand and have a sip. My eyes open wide. "Whoa, this is not just pink lemonade."

"Would you rather the virgin version? That's what I'm drinking."

"Nope, I'm good. You better hope my father doesn't find out you brought booze."

"Sip it slowly."

I acknowledge his warning with a grimace as I take a second, rather large sip. "What's playing?"

"How do you not know? It's all over social media, and I'm pretty sure I saw a flyer in your store window."

I shrug. When the music starts, I get a rush of excitement. "No way!"

He has a wide grin. "Yes, way."

"It's our favourite movie!"

"What is it?" my father asks, confused.

"Pirates of the Caribbean."

"Oh, I was hoping it was a western."

"You won't be disappointed," Sawyer assures him. "It's kind of a western at sea."

I spray myself with enough bug spray that the wind will ensure everyone within a hundred yards behind me will be covered. "Do you remember when this movie came out?"

"Who could forget? Dan Jenkins wore eyeliner to school for a week."

We share a good laugh. "Would you like some popcorn?"

"Not right now, thanks." I hold up my cup. "I have everything I need."

A look of content washes over him. "Stan, is there anything you need?"

"I could use something to drink to wash the taste of bug spray out of my mouth."

I purse my lips. "Sorry, Dad."

Sawyer holds up a ginger ale and a water bottle and then waits for him to choose.

"Thank you," I whisper as everyone settles in to watch the movie.

"For what?"

"Including my dad tonight."

"Of course. I don't mind spending time with him. Growing up, he was a father figure to me."

"It's still really kind of you. And it's not like this is a date, right?" I said it. I've been thinking about it since he asked. At this point, I'm not ashamed to be fishing for answers.

"It's not?" he says, wounded. "Well, that's too bad. I thought it was going well."

I feel my face turn red, and I'm thankful that the darkness hides my blush. When there's a bright scene in the movie that lights up the audience, I catch Sawyer looking at me.

A small child wanders in front of us. Both Sawyer and I look around for a parent. She walks a few feet, then comes back.

"Hi," I say, trying not to scare her. "Where's your mom?" She doesn't answer. Frantically, she looks around in the crowd and then starts to cry.

An announcement comes over the speaker about a lost child, and Sawyer immediately gets to his feet. "Duty calls." He kneels down to her level. "Hey, I'm going to take you to your mom, okay?" He picks her up effortlessly, and she wraps her arms around his neck and holds on tightly. Sawyer puts his phone on speaker and dials. "Hey, I've got her. I'll bring her to the first aid tent."

After stuffing his phone in his pocket, he wipes her tears, leaving smudges of dust across her cheeks. He gives me an apologetic look. "Sorry, I'll be right back."

Something about seeing Sawyer holding a small child tugs at my heart.

"He's a good man," my dad says.

"What?" I say, surprised. He seemed so enthralled in the movie that I didn't think he was aware of what was going on.

"Sawyer. He's a good man."

"I agree."

The night air starts to become cool. When Sawyer returns, he grabs a blanket out of the bag and pulls it over both our legs. "It's getting chilly. I could see my breath on the walk back. Do you think your dad's okay?"

"He should be. He's wearing a heavy sweater and a jacket. But don't worry. He'll let us know if he's cold."

Under the blanket, Sawyers's hand brushes against mine and then lands on top of it. It might be the gin, but I'm not inclined to tug it free. This is the feeling I've been chasing so desperately for the past few years. That comfortable, uncomplicated, totally free kind of happy feeling.

The movie ends too soon, and people rush to gather their belongings and get to their cars. Sawyer takes his time packing up. The night air is still chilly, and goosebumps rise across my skin. Sawyer shakes out the blanket and wraps it around me like a cape. "Better?"

I nod.

"How did you enjoy the movie?" he asks my dad.

"Well, that Johnny Depp fellow is no John Wayne, but I suppose I liked it just fine."

The drive home doesn't take long at all. When we get out of the car, my dad looks tired. Sawyer accompanies us to the door.

My dad puts his hand on Sawyer's shoulder. "Thank you for the night out. I enjoyed myself."

"You're very welcome. I'm glad you came."

"I'll leave you two alone now."

"Thanks, Dad," I say, amused. "You're not going to stand in the front hall and flick the porch lights on and off until I come inside, are you?"

"Goodness, no. If you want to kiss the boy, Grace, invite him in. In fact, invite him to stay over if you want. He can stay in your room."

"Dad!" I say, shocked. "Sawyer and I are just friends."

He waves a dismissive hand. "I know all about friends with benefits, Grace. Do you know how old I am? Nothing shocks me anymore."

Sawyer snickers.

"I won't be entertaining any overnight guests this evening," I assure him.

He shrugs. "Just be sure you're not blaming that on me. That decision is all on you."

I look at Sawyer, feeling completely stunned.

My dad pauses at the doorway. "Let me ask you something, son. Are you planning on sticking around?"

"Yes, Sir. I just accepted a position with the Nottawasaga Conservation Authority."

My eyes widen in excitement. "You did? That's awesome!"

86

My dad nods. "Good. Then kiss the girl goodnight. And make it a good one so she thinks about you all day tomorrow." He closes the door behind him, leaving me with my hands covering my face, completely embarrassed and alone with Sawyer.

Even with my eyes covered, I sense him draw closer. When I lower my hands, I can feel the warmth of his breath on my face. "Sawyer…" I whisper, feeling conflicted.

"Shhh. I think we should listen to your father." He leans in, pressing his mouth against mine in what starts as a featherlike brushing of lips before passion takes over, leaving me weak in the knees and very confused. He takes a step back and smiles before turning and walking away without a word.

I didn't sleep for even a moment last night. My thoughts are so consumed with that kiss that I fumble and drop things all morning. Sawyer has never been one to ignore a challenge. Last night he picked up the gauntlet and rode that bitch to victory.

"Are you sure you're okay?" Sara asks me for the third time.

I squat to stand up a stack of frames I knocked over when I walked past. "Yes, I'm fine. I don't know what's wrong with me today."

The bells on the door jingle as a customer enters the store. When I stand, I find myself face-to-face with Sawyer Kelly.

"Good morning," he says, amused at the sudden flush of pink on my cheeks.

I stumble with my words, and Sara stares at me suspiciously. "Grace?"

"Good morning," I finally force out. "What are you doing here?"

He hands me a spray can. "You forgot your bug spray."

"You came all the way here to return a can of bug spray?" Sara asks.

"No," he admits. "I wanted to ask Grace out for dinner tonight."

Sara pivots on her heels. "I'll leave you two alone."

"How about it?" he asks when she exits the room.

"I can eat," I say, trying to maintain a casual, unaffected appearance.

"Great. What time can I pick you up?"

"Around six?"

"I'll see you then." He turns to leave and then stops at the door. "Oh, and Grace. Just so there's no confusion, this *is* a date."

Sara squeals from the back room. I shake my head, and Sawyer smirks. "See you then."

She peeks into the room when she hears the door to the street close. "I knew it!"

"Okay, calm down."

"I knew there was something there. Why are you not more excited?"

I swallow hard. "I don't know. Last night, he planted a goodbye kiss on me that made my toes curl."

"Oh my! He kissed you?"

I nod my head.

"Is that why you're acting weird this morning?"

"I'm not acting weird. I just…"

"What?"

"It just feels so natural and exciting. But I can't stop thinking it's too good to be true."

Sara frowns. "Grace, you've had so many struggles in your life. Please be open to letting the good things in."

"I'm trying. What happens to our friendship if we explore something further?"

"Would you forgive yourself for not finding out?"

"Every time I let my guard down, something tragic happens, and I have to put the pieces of my heart back together by myself. I don't need a man to look after me or solve my problems."

"I understand that. But this is Sawyer. This is the man you know better than anyone else in this world. I don't believe he'll let you down."

"I've always handled things on my own."

Sara smiles and places a consoling hand on my arm. "But Grace, what if you don't have to? Give him a chance."

"I'm terrified."

"I know. He's your best friend. At the very least, have an open and honest conversation with him about your feelings and your fears."

She's right. "Okay. I will."

"Stop looking so sad. This is a great thing! You should be excited."

"I am. I think."

"Go home. I can handle the shop for the rest of the afternoon."

I hug her. "Thank you, Sara."

"Anything for you. John and I couldn't have children of our own. We always found joy in helping raise our nephews. But, if I could have had a daughter, I would have hoped for one as wonderful as you."

I'm overwhelmed with emotions. "I think you would have been an amazing mother."

"Okay, enough of this mushy stuff. Go home and get your sexy on."

"I'm not sure I have a *sexy* mode."

"You do. Go home and find it."

"Should I, though? I mean, that's not what I'm about. So, it's certainly not what Sawyer finds attractive about me."

"You're right. But go home anyway."

"If I didn't know better, I'd think you're trying to get rid of me. This is the second time this week you've kicked me out of the shop." I pick up my bag and get out my keys.

Sara shrugs. "Stay if you want."

"I'm going." I open the door and almost walk into Jake.

"Where's the fire?" he asks, dodging me.

I stop in my tracks. "There better not be any fires tonight."

He raises a brow. "Huh?"

"Pray there are no fires tonight," I insist.

"Okay." He says, confused.

"I have to go." I push past him, my mind now racing in a thousand directions. I can feel him watching me as I mumble to myself all the way down to the sidewalk.

Chapter Nine

When I arrive home, I find my father in the garden. His eyes are red, and his tear-stained cheeks tell the story.

"Hi, Dad," I say softly. "What's wrong?"

He pulls a tissue out of his pocket and wipes his eyes and nose. "Some days, I just miss her so much."

My heart explodes into a million pieces. "Me too." I sit beside him in silence for a few minutes. "Are you hungry? It's almost dinner time."

"I wouldn't mind a grilled cheese." He blows his nose.

"I can do that. Let's go inside, and I'll put your game shows on."

Without a single word, he stands and follows me to the house. I turn on the television and help him get comfortable. "I'm going into the kitchen to make your sandwich. Are you okay here for a few minutes?"

"Yes," he says, looking at me through bloodshot eyes. "You're coming back to eat with me, right? I don't want to be alone."

It feels like a boulder has just fallen onto my chest. "I'll be here all night. I'm not going anywhere."

"Thank you, Gracie."

I pat his shoulder to reassure him. "I'll be right back. After we eat, we can play a card game if you like."

"That would be wonderful."

I wait until I'm in the kitchen to dial Sawyer's number.

"Hey, what's up? You're not going to cancel on me, are you?"

I sigh as I butter two slices of bread and get out the frying pan. "Actually, I am. But it's not what you think. When I got home, my dad was sitting in the garden crying. He's missing my mom so much today. I can't bring myself to leave him alone tonight."

"Poor guy. He's heartbroken."

"He really is."

"Listen, Grace. Don't worry about it."

"Thank you for understanding. I should go. I promised him a grilled cheese sandwich, and then I'd watch his game shows with him."

"I'm here if you need to talk."

"I'm so sorry."

"Don't be. Dinner happens pretty much every night. We'll just pick another evening."

"You're amazing."

"Not really. Any decent person would do the same."

"Apparently, not all people I meet are decent."

"Are you okay?"

"I'm disappointed about dinner and really concerned about my dad."

"I'll check in later. Go spend time with him."

"I will."

My dad is yelling answers at the television as I place his sandwich in front of him on the coffee table. It warms my heart to see him sitting on the edge of his chair and enjoying his show.

"Can you believe this guy didn't know the answer?" He picks up his grilled cheese and devours it.

"Do you want another sandwich?"

"Shhhhh!"

"Sorry!" I can't believe he just shushed me. I look down at a romance novel on the coffee table. "Where did this come from?" I pick it up and read the cover. "The Firefighters Flame. Sounds steamy." It's unfortunate that there's no one to appreciate my sense of humour.

I wait for a commercial break. "Hey, Dad. Do you know where this book came from?"

He squints. "It's your mother's."

"Mom read this kind of stuff?" I ask, surprised.

"All the time. Your mom loved to read. Especially love stories."

That's interesting since I never saw my mom read. "Okay, but where did it come from, and how did it end up on the table today?"

"I have no idea." He waves his hand at me when the show resumes. I guess I'm waiting for the next commercial break before I can talk again.

The doorbell rings, and I'm a little on edge because I'm not expecting anyone. Reluctantly, I go to the front door and stand there, listening for voices or something to identify the visitor. Should I just turn out the lights and pretend we're not home? Or would that encourage home invaders?

"Grace? It's me; open the door. My hands are full."

"Sawyer?" I unlock the door and pull it open. "What are you doing here?"

"I thought you could use some moral support. I brought pizza." He hands me the box. "And the rest of the gin."

"You really know what a girl needs."

"I'm sorry; I would have messaged or called to let you know I was here, but I couldn't find my phone. I think it might have flown off the truck seat and onto the floor. Hello Stan!" he yells as we pass the living room on the way to the kitchen.

"Don't even bother until the end of his show. He's laser-focused on the last round."

"My parents get like that watching game shows too! And I'm certain that the shows they watch are reruns they've seen ten or fifteen times, but they just keep on yelling at the television as if they're expecting a different outcome this time."

I laugh as I get out a couple of plates. Sawyer opens a cupboard and takes out two glasses.

"You remember which one is the glass cupboard?"

"People seldom change the cupboard contents around. We drank a lot of lemonade in your backyard."

I place a slice of pizza on each plate. "We sure did. Remember the time we forgot to add the sugar?"

"My mouth was puckered for hours."

"It made my eyes water."

Sawyer puts ice in the bottom of the glasses and then tips the bottle of gin. I raise my brow. "A little over-generous on the pour if you're not trying to get into my panties."

Sawyer smirks.

"Are we drinking it neat?"

"You don't have to drive anywhere, do you?"

"No, but you do."

"It's one drink. Unless you're throwing me out in the next hour, I'll be fine. And if I'm not, I will call Ben or take a cab. I wouldn't gamble with my life."

"Well then. Cheers!" I lift the glass to my mouth, and the first sip burns all the way down, making my eyes water.

Sawyer whistles as he places his down on the table.

"There's cranberry juice in the fridge."

"Good idea," he admits. "I'm not sure it will water it down enough. I might have to split it into two glasses."

I cautiously take a sip. "I think this is okay now."

"Are you sure? Or did that first swig melt all the nerves in your mouth?"

"It's good," I assure him.

I hear the closing music for the game show. "Let's go say hello now." I grab my pizza and glass of gin.

Sawyer follows me into the other room. "Hello Stan," he says again.

"Hello, Sawyer. When did you get here?" he asks confused.

"Just a little while ago, sir."

"Come and sit down."

"Thank you." Sawyer sits on the couch beside him. I can see the amused look on his face as he pushes the romance novel to the side and places down his food and drink.

"It's not mine," I clarify.

Sawyer grins. "I'm not judging."

I change the subject. "Would you like some pizza, Dad?"

"No, thank you. Every time I eat pizza, I get heartburn."

"Me too," Sawyer adds.

I squint at him. "Then why did you buy it?"

He shrugs. "It tastes good, and it's cheap."

I take a deck of cards out of the drawer in the coffee table and place them down in front of him. "Did you ever learn how to play any decent card games?"

"What?" he says, offended. "Crazy Eights isn't a decent card game?"

"Barely, but you lost every game."

He grins, and his brown eyes twinkle.

"No! Are you saying you let me win?"

"I admit nothing."

"Why would you do that?" I pick up the nearest throw cushion and launch it at him. He grabs his drink and ducks.

"Dad, do you want to play a game of cards?"

"No, it's getting late. I'm going to go to bed. You kids play if you want." He shuffles down the hall and closes his door. I look at my watch. It's only eight o'clock.

"Do you want to play crazy eights?" Sawyer waggles his eyebrows.

"I want another drink."

He picks up the deck of cards and hands them to me. "You shuffle and deal. I'll get us another drink."

I deal out the hand, stewing over his silent confession. When he returns with the drinks, I give him the evil eye.

"Whoa, what happened while I was out of the room? I was only gone a few minutes."

I take a large swig of my drink.

His eyes open wide. "You might…want to…sip this one."

I start to cough.

"It's a little bit stronger. Do you want me to dump it out and make you another one?"

"No!" I say defiantly as I pick it up and take another long drink.

Sawyer picks up his cards and glances at me nervously.

"You will NOT let me win this game," I demand.

A sudden look of understanding washes over him. "I promise."

The next hour turns into an unintended drinking game. Sawyer wins a hand, and I drink. After twelve consecutive losses, I swish my arm across the table, sending the cards flying through the room.

"Had enough?" he asks smugly.

I get to my feet, feeling the weight of the gin. Sawyer reacts quickly, standing and steadying me. "You kicked my ass in crazy eights. My entire childhood was a lie."

Sawyer chuckles. "Where are you going?"

"I have an idea. Follow me."

"Where are we going?"

"Outside. Put on your shoes."

"I'm not sure that's a good idea, Grace."

"I'm a little buzzed. I need some fresh air. Are you coming?"

"Against my better judgement."

I search through the front closet for the flashlight but the gin has made me tipsy. I hate that feeling.

Sawyer opens the door and makes sure I navigate the few small steps down to the driveway. "Where are we going?"

"I need to get something out of the garage."

Sawyer lifts the door, and it makes a loud, rusty grinding noise.

"Shhh," I giggle.

"What do you need? I'll get it for you."

"It's okay, I know exactly where it is."

Sawyer looks nervous.

"I found it." I hand him the box. "My Dad bought that for you and me."

"Chalk?" he asks confused. "In case we find a body?"

"No!" I scowl. "Why would your mind even go there?"

He laughs. "The gin."

I take the box from him and take out a brand-new piece of white chalk. "We're going to play hopscotch."

"Now? It's almost eleven o'clock. It's dark. How will we even see the boxes?"

"Afraid?"

"Yes. Very much. You could get hurt."

I ignore him and squat down to draw the hopscotch board on the driveway, trying not to tip over.

"We're really doing this, huh?"

"Yup." The cool evening air is sobering.

"I'll look for some rocks."

I trace over the board several times, ensuring the outline is dark enough.

Sawyer returns from the darkness of the front yard. "Okay, this is the best I could find."

"What have you got?"

"A rock and...something else."

I look at the bizarre item in his hand. "What is that? It's not a rock."

"I don't know. I found it in the garden."

"Is that skunk feces?"

He drops it as if it's on fire, and I burst out into laughter. "I'm kidding, it's a pinecone." I bend down and pick it up.

Still feeling suspicious, he closes his hand around the rock. "That one is yours," he announces.

Playing hopscotch after so many years has its own challenges. Add nightfall and alcohol, and it takes it to a whole new level of bad ideas. We navigate the first few levels without much difficulty, but when I get to the higher square, I suddenly feel lightheaded. I begin to tip to one side, and Sawyer grabs for me as I fall full force into his arms. Every sense seems heightened. I can feel the rise and fall of his muscular chest against me. He's wearing the same cologne he wore in high school. I look up into his eyes, and my gaze locks on his. Our lips are so close that the moonlight barely shines through our silhouettes. All I can think about is that last kiss. The anticipation of another makes my heart beat faster.

"Are you okay?" he asks after a long moment.

"I am." I try to gather my thoughts as I stand on my own two feet and put some distance between us. "I think I'm done with hopscotch for the night."

"Thank the Lord. I'm not sure why we're doing this."

I shrug and feel a little sad as the effects of the alcohol wear off. "I just wanted to recreate the happy times we had when we were kids."

He takes my hand, leads me to the porch step and sits.

"Sawyer. Can I ask you something?"

"Of course."

"What's happening between us? What are we doing?"

"I think we're sobering up."

"That's not what I mean."

"I know."

"What is this? Something is shifting. Do you feel it, too?"

He reaches for my hand. "Yes."

"Could there be something more here than just a friendship?"

He gently tugs on my hand and reels me in closer between his knees, and we are face to face. "Would that be a bad thing?"

"Honestly? I don't know. I've been thinking about it. I think my feelings for you are growing in a romantic way."

He lets out a sigh of relief. "I feel the same way. I was worried that kiss might have scared you away."

"No, if anything, that kiss forced me to realize how I'm feeling."

He grins. "It was a great kiss," he brags.

"What do we do now?"

He pulls me in closer and puts his hands on my hips. "I think we explore our feelings and let things happen naturally."

"I'm afraid. The other night, I had dreams about the day you left for Alberta."

"As long as you still want me here, I'm not going anywhere. I'm home." He tugs me the rest of the way until I'm firmly planted against his chest. With a gentle touch of his hand, he sweeps my hair away from my face. His thumb traces along my jaw and then over my lips. "So many times I've thought about these lips."

My stomach flutters, and I squeeze my thighs together, trying to settle an ache that's growing. When he leans in and claims my lips, I feel weak. I return his kiss with the same growing passion until my quiet moans of pleasure echo in the cool night air. Steam rises from the heat of our breath when we break for air.

"Why do you think nothing happened between us back then?"

He shrugs. "Remember the night we went to that party out in Shelburne, and we got storm stayed?"

"I do. Biggest blizzard of the year."

"That night, you and I talked for hours."

"That was normal for us."

"I don't know what it was that night, but something *clicked* for me."

I lower my brow. "What do you mean?"

"You went to bed in one of the spare rooms upstairs, and I couldn't sleep. I went upstairs and stood outside the door, wanting to come in and tell you about my feelings. I must have stood there for more than half an hour."

"Why didn't you?"

"I didn't know if you were feeling the same. The following morning came, and the roads were clear. Life went back to normal. I didn't see any evidence that your feelings for me were anything more than platonic. So, when the opportunity came in the spring, I moved to Alberta."

My eyes well up with tears. "I always thought you moved because you didn't care about me anymore."

"No. No, the exact opposite. I left because I cared more than I should have."

I force a small smile. "I didn't know." Our peaceful confession is interrupted by the howling of coyotes. "That sounds a little too close for comfort. We should go in the house."

"Actually, Grace. I have training really early in the morning. I should get going home."

"Absolutely NOT! You've been drinking. You'll stay here in the spare room."

"I don't want to be any trouble."

"It's not. My father gives me enough things to worry about. I don't need to worry about you going home this late at night and being eaten by coyotes or bears."

He raises a brow. "I don't think there's been any bear sightings in Mono Mills to worry about."

"Maybe not yet. I'm not taking no for an answer."

"Okay, but I'm not going to wake you in the morning when I leave. I have to be up at five A.M."

"That's only a few hours away!"

He gets to his feet and picks up the flashlight. "I better see if I can find my phone so I can set the alarm."

I watch as he opens his truck door and leans in, searching the floor. "Got it!"

He closes the door with a slam and then runs toward me. I'm startled by the look on his face. "What's wrong?"

"Get in the house! Go! Go! Go!"

I turn and rush up the steps. "What's wrong?"

"Angry skunk!"

"What?"

I turn as I get to the door and see her shooting out of the darkness like a fur torpedo. Her fur puffed out, and looking angry. I pull the door open just as Sawyer reaches the top step. He pushes me through the doorway and pulls it shut behind him.

Inside, he holds his chest as he tries to catch his breath. "I studied wildlife behaviours, and I had no idea skunks could get that aggressive."

I start to snicker, and then it turns into a full-blown hard laugh. Tears start rolling down my cheeks. "Did you get your phone?"

He holds up his hand. "Yes."

I pull myself together and wipe the tears of laughter from my eyes. My stomach muscles are cramping from laughing so hard. "You better get some sleep." He follows me up the stairs and down the hall to the spare room. There's an awkward moment at the doorway I'm eager to put an end to. "Good night. Let me know if there's anything you need."

I go to my room and close the door. I toss and turn restlessly for what seems like hours. My body is thrumming with unmet needs. All I can think is that Sawyer is in the room next door. Fuck it. I throw the blankets to the side and get out of bed. When I pull the door open, Sawyer is standing there shirtless and with his jeans undone.

"Hi." He says in a low voice.

"Hi. Are you going to come in this time?"

"Only if you want me to."

I stand to the side and welcome him in. His body brushes against me in a teasing manner.

He joins me in bed, and after a passionate moment of kissing, he shifts his weight, forcing me to my back as his heavily muscled body presses me into the mattress. I'm void of all rational thought and lost in a sensual storm of emotion. A smile quirks at the corner of his lips as he slides his boxers down, freeing his erection. My hands skim along his sides and over his hips until I can grip his perfectly taut bare ass and express my appreciation with a small intake of breath.

Sawyer stops, and the anticipation makes me squirm with growing needs.

"Grace," he whispers.

"What's wrong?" I ask, straining to see his face.

"Maybe this isn't the right time for this."

Sawyer has always been chivalrous, but I want his mouth on me more than anything I've ever wanted before.

"It's been an emotional day, and you've been drinking."

I'm painfully aware, yet this, with Sawyer, is exactly what I need right now. I acknowledge his concern and then reassure him. "I want this."

He shakes his head. "Believe me, so do I. But we don't need to rush into it."

"Waiting is what fucked everything up the first time," I say with a shaky voice.

He presses his lips to my forehead. "I never want to be a source of regret for you. It can wait."

I rake my fingers through his hair and then guide him in for a kiss. "You are the one thing I have never regretted in my life. What I need right now is *YOU*."

His conflicted look fades as he concedes. Sucking a nipple into his mouth with a hard pull, he draws desire from every dark corner of my soul. Skillful hands quickly have me dripping with desire and on the edge. I spread my legs to accommodate the rugged width of his hips and invite him in. Sawyer firmly grasps one wrist at a time and holds them over my head, making me a willing captive of his dominance.

Nibbling and nipping from my shoulder to the base of my neck, he makes me squirm. "Open your eyes and look at me," he whispers in a feral growl that vibrates over my skin. When our eyes lock together, I brace myself for his possession. His first thrust makes me gasp. Sawyer controls his pace, bringing me to that place where all thoughts halt, and there's nothing but pleasure. It's the driving force behind his every action. I tilt my hips, trying to force him deeper, and fall victim to an overload of sensations as I begin erupting and tingling. Sawyer convulses as his warm release pulses inside me, and our already entangled souls fuse together as one.

Chapter Ten

I open my eyes when Sawyer brushes a goodbye kiss on my lips. "I'll call you later," he whispers.

Completely exhausted, I drift back to sleep.

I startle awake a few hours later at the sound of clattering in the kitchen. "I'll be right down, Dad," I holler on my way to the shower. I can still smell his cologne as I turn on the water and let the warmth surround me. It's a welcome reminder of last night. I shower and dress and rush down the stairs. I stop in my tracks as I find my father standing in the kitchen washing dishes. "Hi."

"Good morning!" he says cheerfully. "I see you had a guest last night."

My face turns crimson red. "Yes. He had to leave early to start training for his new position."

He stops scrubbing and pauses, then turns to me with a serious expression. "Are you happy, Grace?"

"I am. But this is very new territory for Sawyer and me. I don't know how everything will work out." I pick up the dish towel and start drying.

"If it's meant to be, it will all work out. Your mother always thought you two would end up together."

"She did?"

"She watches over you, and I know she's very happy for you. That's all we ever wanted for you, Grace. To be happy."

"Thanks, Dad. I love you."

"I love you too."

"Dad, I was thinking about gathering up some gardening tools and heading over to Sawyer's place. He's so busy I thought it would be a nice gesture if we helped him out by doing a little work in the garden."

He rings out the dishcloth and hangs it over the faucet. "I'll get my hat."

When I come out of the yard with an arm full of rakes and tools, he's already sitting in the passenger seat of my car.

"Ready?" I ask as I climb in beside him.

"Ready," he confirms.

"You might not be ready when you see what we're dealing with."

"How bad can it be?"

"I'll let you decide for yourself."

It's not a very long drive up the highway before we reach the gravel road that leads to Sawyers property. "Do you know any of the history of the town of Mono?" I ask curiously.

"No. But I know there are some historical plaques around the area that pay homage to some of the original settlers. There are quite a few preserved historical landmarks."

I pull into the driveway and park. My dad looks around at the surrounding wild jungle and looks at me, overwhelmed. "I changed my mind. Let's go home."

I laugh, pleased to see him in such good spirits.

"Just kidding. Let's get to work."

"Where do we start?"

"I would start in the front garden so the house looks a little more welcoming when you pull up."

"Good plan."

I gather the tools out of the back of my car and drop them in a pile on the front lawn.

"Most of this is just overgrown. If we pull all this dead stuff from last year's blooms out of the garden, it will make a big difference."

My phone rings, and I smile as I answer. "Hi!"

"Good morning. What are you doing?"

"Nothing. Just hanging out with my dad."

"Oh. Not doing anything special?"

"No, just hanging out."

Sawyer chuckles. "Grace, I can see you on my security camera feed."

I curse, and my father looks up, shocked at my language.

"Well, that sucks. Dad and I were going to surprise you by helping out a little."

"That's a very welcome gesture. Thank you. I'll be home in a few hours. Don't let your dad overdo it, okay? I know we forget sometimes, but he's over seventy."

"I'll make sure he doesn't over-exert himself. He's in his element right now, raking all the dead things out of the garden."

"I'll take all the help I can get. See you soon."

I hang up the phone and look around for the camera. When I spot it and the flashing red light, I make a funny face in hopes of making Sawyer laugh. As my dad rakes, I scoop up the dead roughage and stuff it into a paper sack. It doesn't take long before we're done, and I'm shocked at the difference it makes.

"There's a fire pit over there. Do you want me to start a fire and burn up all these dead leaves?"

I hesitate. "I'm not sure if he has a fire permit yet. We better leave it for him to deal with."

"Fire permit," he grumbles. "Back in the day if you had stuff to burn you just burned it. Isn't he a volunteer firefighter? Shouldn't that get him a free pass?"

"I don't know, but he can deal with it. There's another spot I want your help with." I hand him a water bottle. "How's your energy level? Are you getting tired?"

"I'm fine."

"Good, come with me." I walk around the side of the house and down the pathway toward the small outbuilding. "There's a garden spot down here that's surrounded by bushes. I'm not sure what they are." I walk slowly, making sure that he can keep up.

He stops and looks all around us. "Well, isn't that something?"

"Pretty spot, isn't it?"

"It is. These over here are rose bushes."

"What are these?" I ask, walking to a cluster of leaves a few feet away.

"I believe those are hydrangeas." He looks up at the sky. "Once the summer sun gives them several hours of light a day, they will have magnificent blooms."

"I know these bushes! These are raspberries."

"Yes, they are. Be careful. They're prickly."

"They go all the way down the fence line as far as I can see."

"I imagine somebody spent a lot of time in this garden."

"Me too. Should I pull these weeds out?"

He walks toward me and gives them a closer look. "I don't think those are weeds. It looks like Bee Balm to me."

"What's Bee Balm?"

"It's a perennial flower that's very popular with pollinators."

"This is why I asked you to come. I would have pulled it all out."

"It's already in bloom. Soon enough, the hummingbirds will be coming around looking for its nectar."

"So, how do I know what's a flower and what's a weed?"

"Well, the easy answer is, if you don't recognize the plant, just wait. If you like what it looks like when it blooms, then it's a flower. If you don't like it, it's a weed. Pull it out."

"So, I need to be patient."

"An unfamiliar term to your generation." He pulls a hankie out of his pocket and wipes sweat from his brow.

"Where's your hat?"

"I guess I left it in the car."

"I'll go get it for you. We should take a break. I think it's almost lunchtime anyway."

"Actually, Grace. Can you take me home?"

"Of course. Are you okay?"

"Just a little overheated, and it's making me tired."

When he gets in the car, I turn on the air conditioning to help him cool down faster. "Thanks for helping me today."

"You're welcome."

I pull out onto the highway and hit the gas. "I can't believe how busy this road has become."

"It's now the major connecting highway between two large cities."

Sawyer calls. "Hey."

"Hi. I'm just taking Dad home. But I guess you already know that."

"Actually, I haven't been watching you all morning, but it was tempting. How is he?"

"He says he's overheated and tired."

"Make sure you keep him hydrated."

"Will do."

"So, I won't see you when I get home."

"You sound disappointed."

"A little. I was looking forward to seeing you. I hated rushing off this morning."

"I'd say I hated it too. But I was exhausted. I went right back to sleep."

Sawyer laughs. "I have to go. My break is over."

"Let me get Dad settled, and maybe I'll meet you at the house later."

"Okay. Got to run."

I park the car and help Dad into the house. While he searches for his game show on the television, I unpack the lunch I took on the coffee table. "This is a lovely picnic," he says, delighted. After half a sandwich, he turns off his show and heads to his room. I pick up the novel that magically appeared and begin to read through it. I don't know if I should be amused or traumatized that my mother dog eared the naughty pages for future reference. A short while later my dad comes out of his room.

"Feeling better after a little rest?"

"Much better. You go back to Sawyer's, Grace. I'm going to spend some time out in the garden."

"Are you sure? I can ask Sawyer to come here if you'd rather I stay home."

"Nonsense. You stayed home with me last night. I'll be fine. I'll call you if I need anything."

He doesn't wait for an answer. Or even a discussion. He just walks out the side door and leaves me sitting with my dirty book in hand. I place it on the table and walk to the kitchen window to make sure, one last time, that he's okay.

The traffic on the highway is insanely aggressive at this time of day. Commuters come in and go out of the Orangeville area, and everyone is in a hurry. I'm thankful to turn onto the peaceful rural road. I don't message Sawyer to let him know I'm back because he already knows.

I rake the front yard until my hands begin to blister. In the warmest part of the day, I search for a place to rest and escape the heat. Once again, I'm drawn down the pathway and find a place to sit on a log at the edge of the forest. I imagine it's a seldomly appreciated view of the garden. The day is quiet, and the breeze is light. A thrumming sound, followed by the vibration of air on my cheek, heightens my awareness of my surroundings. A few inches from my face, a hummingbird pauses to assess the garden before deciding the sweet nectar would be bountiful. I have never seen one so close, not even in our own garden, and I'm humbled at how his diminutive size projects such grand beauty.

Bee balm and gladiolas stand high and proud in the garden. They wave in the gentle breeze, releasing their flowery scent into the warm air. As my father predicted, the hummingbird hovers over petals and, with his long beak, drinks from each flower. I reach for my phone but don't take it from my pocket. I am so enthralled with the idea that I am the only one to witness this moment in time that I want to see it in real life and not through a lens. I pay little attention to the rustling of leaves from the bush a few feet away. As the tiny bird moves from flower to flower, its wings flutter at such a great speed they can only be heard and not seen. I feel such a strong connection, and I wonder if it's possible its majestic presence is a sign or message that I need to acknowledge. As I contemplate what the universe might be trying to tell me, my view becomes a flash of grey and white, and I discover I'm not alone, as shimmering emerald-green feathers are plucked from the air by fangs and fur. I gasp. A rather pudgy feline walks toward me, proud of her accomplishment. I frown as she sits in front of me with a tiny emerald-green tail protruding from her mouth. "Oh, kitty. What did you do?" With a grin the Cheshire cat would be proud of, she makes a throaty noise, leans forward, and spits it out at my feet.

I clasp my hand over my mouth as she turns on stubby legs, sashays her plump middle straight into the long grass, and disappears.

"I'll get a shovel."

"SAWYER!!!" I scream.

"Sorry, did I startle you?"

My heart races at a concerning rate. "You have to stop doing that to me."

He chuckles as he scoops the poor dead hummingbird onto the end of the shovel. I follow him to the old gravestone and watch as he digs a small hole and covers it in dirt.

"That seems like an appropriate spot to bury it. I don't understand why she killed it but didn't eat it."

"Did you see the size of that cat? It hasn't missed many meals. I'm sure it was hunting out of instinct, not hunger."

"I think I'm traumatized."

"I'm glad that didn't happen while your dad was here."

My eyes open wide. "Me too!"

"Grace, watch where you're walking. I saw a piece of chicken wire out here the other day, and I meant to pick it up."

Before I know it I'm laying face down in the muddy pathway. "Thanks, I found it."

"Are you okay?" He helps me to my feet and tries to knock some of the dirt off.

"I think you're going to have to hose me off."

"Not a chance. Follow me to the house."

I pry my shoes off at the front door and hesitate.

"Don't worry about tracking mud through the house."

I follow him up the stairs and into the bathroom.

I'm shocked at the size of the room. "Oh, this is a surprise."

"Don't get too excited. The shower doesn't work at the moment. The plumber is coming tomorrow."

"That's okay. Look at the size of that tub."

He puts the stop in the drain and turns on the water, adjusting it until I can see the steam from the heat. "I'll bring up clean towels." He glances over his shoulder on his way out of the room. "It's big enough for two. In case you're wondering."

I quickly strip out of my muddy clothes and climb in. I wasn't wondering, but now I can't stop thinking about it. If I don't stop thinking about it, I'll have to turn on the cold water. I scrub the dirt off my face and arms and lean back to rinse my hair. There's a quick knock on the door. "Grace? I brought you a towel. Are you almost done?"

"I am."

He pushes open the door and walks in. I suppose I shouldn't feel self-conscious after last night. He holds the towel open in front of him, and I get to my feet. As I step over the edge of the tub, he wraps the soft, warm towel around me. "Did you warm this up in the dryer?"

"I did."

Who does that, other than in the movies? "I thought you might have joined me," I say as he hands me another towel to dry my hair.

"I was tempted."

I stop rubbing the dampness from my hair and look at him in the mirror. "Why didn't you?"

"I thought we should save some of the fun things for the second week of dating."

"That's a good point. I'm looking forward to it. So, are we defining this relationship now? Are we officially dating?"

"We are. Any objections?"

"None. I'm rather enjoying the perks."

He watches me from the doorway, studying my body and every curve. "I put out clothes on the end of my bed that would probably fit you."

"Thanks."

"Last door at the end of the hall."

I try to ignore his commanding presence, but I can feel the heat of his stare. My pulse begins to quicken as I try to pass him in the doorway, and he places his hand across the threshold, stopping me. I turn to face him, causing the towel to tug loose and slide to the floor.

"A hummingbird?" He skims his fingertips across it. The whirling emotions inside me stifle all hopes of speaking coherent words.

"Aren't you full of surprises? I didn't think you were the tattoo type." His lips come dangerously close to mine as his hands slide down my warm, damp skin. Without warning, he lifts me into his arms with little effort and carries me in a few long strides to his room.

He gently tosses me on the bed, then strips off his clothes and discards them on the floor. As he joins me in the bed, a sudden awakening takes place inside of me. I run my hands up his muscular chest as he parts his lips, and his warm tongue slips inside, teasing and deepening the kiss until I begin to feel lightheaded. He allows me a quick exchange of breath before claiming my mouth again.

As we lay here tangled together, a stimulating charge courses through my body. Suddenly, I am the bonfire, and he is the gasoline.

Chapter Eleven

It's Saturday afternoon, and the store is buzzing with people.

"How's your dad doing?" Sara asks as she straightens a display of candles.

"You know, we haven't had any more incidents. It's kind of amazing."

"That's great to hear. I read an article where an elderly woman started acting strangely, and her family finally figured out that she was getting her meds confused. She was taking double the dosage of something that caused similar symptoms to dementia. Maybe his meds were out of whack?"

"It's possible."

"Tell me how it's going with Sawyer," she insists.

"It's good."

She scowls. "I want details. It's been a couple of weeks. What's it like? Do you have any regrets?"

"Not one. Our friendship hasn't changed at all. And he's amazing with my dad."

"Have you had sex with him?"

I look around the crowded room, feeling embarrassed. "Can we talk about this later?" I whisper.

Her face lights up, and she squeals. "You have!"

"Shhhh! There are people everywhere in here."

"Excuse me," a lady in an expensive coat interrupts us. "I'm looking for something unique for my front foyer."

Sara directs her to the back of the store. "We have some unique reclaimed furniture pieces over here. I'm sure there's something for you."

When Sara rejoins me, she looks haggard. "Good Lord, it's only lunchtime."

"Tell me about it. If this is going to be the normal traffic, I think we can safely afford to hire someone for weekends," I say, slipping my sore feet out of my shoes to soothe them on the cool cement floor.

"That's amazing because I'm exhausted."

"Me too. And I hate leaving my dad alone on weekends."

Sara straightens one of the displays. "We've sold out of the replica weathervanes again."

"I thought there were more in the back. I'll text the supplier and see how soon she can have more ready. Hopefully, Jake will have more treasures for us soon. His work is so popular it flies out of here."

"I'll go back and look for things we can put out." Sara heads to the storeroom.

"Excuse me, miss. Could I get some help here, please?"

I smile and turn to find Sawyer standing behind me with a pizza.

"That depends on what kind of help you need, sir. I'm not going to lie. If it's anything other than helping you to eat

122

that pizza, I'm going to be disappointed." His phone alarm screeches to life, making me jump and knock over a display. "Geez, Sawyer, that thing is going to give me a heart attack yet."

"I'm sorry, I'm on call," he apologizes as he hands me the pizza and then pulls it out of his pocket to read the alert. Sudden terror washes over his expression.

"What is it?" Sara asks as she joins us.

"Fire," he confirms. "Grace..."

I raise my brow, waiting for him to expand. "Sawyer? What is it?"

"I need to go. *Now*."

Something isn't right. "Wait! What's going on." I follow him to the door. "Sawyer!" I grab his coat, and he stops. "Tell me what's going on."

"There's a fire at your house. Stay here. I'll call you when I get there. I have to go."

My stomach drops. "The fire is at my house?" I gasp. "I'm coming with you."

"I don't think that's a good idea," Sara adds, looking at Sawyer with a concerned look.

"I agree. Stay put, Grace."

"If you think I'm staying here, you're both nuts. And we're wasting time. My father is there."

Sensing my panic, Sawyer gives in. "Okay, you can come, but I'm driving."

I practically run to his truck and buckle in. The ten-minute drive feels like two hours. Sawyer shows his identification to the officer blocking the road so he can gain access. Watching the flames as the black smoke darkens the sky, I open the door and ignore the officer's request to get back in the car.

"Grace!" Sawyer yells as the cruiser moves, and he begins to pull forward through the blockade. "GRACE!"

Adrenaline overcomes me, and I run toward the house. Sawyer squeals to a stop as close as he can and runs after me. A tall firefighter in full gear intercepts me. I struggle to get past him, but he's stronger and just as determined. Sawyer reaches us, still calling my name.

"Are you crazy!" he yells through panted breaths. "You don't run into an open fire."

"My father!" I cry out. "He's in there."

"You don't know that. Let's check with the commander before we panic."

I try to calm my reaction, but I'm shaking. Sawyer holds me firmly. "Okay? Let's get information first. Okay? Promise me you won't try to go into the house."

I hesitate. Lost in a world of confusion. Smoke and heat overwhelm me as the crackling fire engulfs what used to be my family home.

"Come with me. Let's calm down." Sawyer searches the crowd of scrambling firefighters for a familiar face. "Rose!" He walks us toward a female firefighter quenching her thirst at the back of one of the vehicles.

"Sawyer." She wipes the sweat from her brow, leaving a dark streak of ash and dirt across her face.

"This is Grace. This is her house."

"I'm sorry we couldn't do more. When we got here, the flames were already through the roof."

I feel nauseous. "My dad? He was home. Is he okay? Did he get out?" I blurt out.

She tugs off her helmet and points in the direction of an ambulance as the back doors close. "They're taking him to the hospital. He's suffering from smoke inhalation. He was calling out for someone named Dorothy. He was so frantic and confused we didn't know for sure if someone was in the house or not."

"There was no one else home," Sawyer confirms as he steps in front of the ambulance, forcing them to stop.

"I'll let the commander know." Rose grabs her helmet and heads back into the chaos.

The ambulance driver rolls down the window. "Sawyer. What's going on?"

"This is Grace. You have her dad in the back. She wants to accompany him to the hospital."

He jumps out and opens the door. Sawyer kisses me on the top of the head before helping me in. "I'll meet you there in a little while."

"Thank you," I say, feeling distraught.

He nods.

The paramedic closes the door behind me. "He'll be glad to see you. He had us concerned you were in the house."

I sit beside him and reach for his hand. "Dad, I'm here. Can you hear me?"

His eyes flutter open. "Grace?"

"Yes, Dad, it's me."

"I'm sorry, Grace. I'm so sorry. I burnt down the house."

He breaks into a hard sob, and I squeeze his hand tightly. "It's okay. All that matters is that you're safe."

"Everything is gone," he sobs, gripping my hand as hard as he can. "Your mother is gone."

I brush my hand across his cheek, trying to calm him. I'm completely heartbroken to see him like this. "It's okay. It's just a house." But it's not just a house. It's the house he and my mother bought when they were first married. It's the house where they raised their only daughter. Every memory of my childhood, family memento and cherished keepsake of my mother was in that house, and now everything is gone.

Sawyer quietly enters the hospital room a few hours later. "I'm sorry," he whispers. "I called earlier, and the nurse said he was stable and resting, so I stayed to help the fire crew."

"It's okay. He's been drifting in and out."

"How is he?"

"The doctor says he's out of danger. They're going to keep him on oxygen overnight and monitor his vitals. The stress of this kind of event can be the more dangerous consideration at his age."

"I'll stay with you."

"Thank you, but there isn't anything you can do. I'm going to sleep beside him in case he wakes up and needs anything. I don't want him to wake up alone in the middle of the night."

"I agree, that would be traumatic."

"Especially since he's already having periods of confusion."

Sawyer reaches for my hand with a sympathetic look. "I'm sorry, Grace."

I'm suddenly overcome with emotion. "I'm just thankful that he's okay. I shouldn't have left him alone."

"Don't do that to yourself. This isn't your fault."

I take a deep breath and try to stop my bottom lip from quivering.

"Are you sure you don't want me to stay?"

I wipe the escaping tears from beneath my eyes with the pad of my thumb. "I'm sure."

Sawyer wraps his arms around me and squeezes tightly. "If you need me, no matter what time of the night, you call me. I'll come back."

He places a finger beneath my chin and gently forces me to raise my head. His sympathetic look almost causes my emotional floodgate to open. "Promise me you'll call if you need me."

"I promise," I say through a strained voice.

He presses a tender kiss on my lips. "I'll be back first thing in the morning."

I watch him walk to the door, wanting to call for him to stay. I don't.

My eyes close, and I feel exhaustion gaining control. It's been a long, restless night waking up every time my father moves or makes a noise. I would have thought a hospital would be calm and quiet during the twilight hours, but there's an endless barrage of people up and down the hall.

It feels like I've just fallen asleep when I hear Sawyer whispering my name. I open my eyes to find him crouching beside me with an extra-large tea. I sit straight up, giving my full attention to the monitors. Relieved they're still beeping and moving, I relax and take the tea out of Sawyer's hand.

"Thank you."

He smiles and nods. "How was his night?"

"Uneventful. He seemed to have a peaceful sleep."

"I imagine they gave him something to assist with that. How about you? How are you?"

I twist my head from one side to the next, trying to work out the kinks. "I don't think I had a very deep sleep. Every time something beeped, it startled me awake."

"I bet."

My dad's lashes begin to flutter, and he calls out. "Dorothy?"

Sawyer's brow creases as he frowns.

"Dad, it's me, Grace. I'm here." My heart aches as I go to his side.

His eyes open wide, and he looks around the room frantically until he's had a moment to remember where he is. "I dreamt I saw your mother. She looked as beautiful as the day I met her." His eyes revert to Sawyer. He squints, then looks over at me for an explanation.

I smile. "Sawyer came to make sure you're okay."

"I thought he moved away."

I frown, saddened by his confusion. Sawyer moves to my side. "I've moved back to town."

"That's good. Real good."

The door swings open, making me jump. "Doctor Fulton," I say, placing my hand on my chest.

"Call me Grant."

It's not hard to smile when he's in the room. Despite his intense professionalism, he is ruggedly handsome and charming. Sawyer raises a brow at my reaction to him.

He reaches for Sawyer's hand, and something strange passes between them. "Good to see you again. When did you get back into town?"

I raise a brow and listen attentively to the exchange.

"A couple of months ago."

Grant places a hand on Sawyer's shoulder. "I'm sorry to hear about your aunt. I wasn't on duty the night she came in, but I'm sure they did everything they could."

"Thank you. Don't sweat it. She was ninety, and her quality of life had been deteriorating for months."

"Now, let's talk about this patient."

"How is he doing?" I ask anxiously.

"Everything seems fine. Oxygen levels are normal. His heart has a little anomaly, but otherwise, it seems strong."

"It's broken," I say sadly.

"Broken?"

"Since my mom passed away."

He gives me a sympathetic look. "Gotcha." He looks over the data on the screens and looks for updates on the charts. "How are you feeling, Stanley?"

"I'm tired. Just very tired."

I reach over and hold his hand.

Grant writes a few notes on the clipboard while he talks. "Did you fall or hit your head trying to get out of the house?"

"No. Everything went black, and then I remember being on the ground. Dorothy pulled me out."

I swallow hard. "I'm sure it was one of the fire and rescue people that got you out, Dad."

He stares at me as if I've just told him there's no such thing as Santa. Sawyer reaches up and gently presses on my shoulder, suggesting I let it go. Grant glances between us.

"Well, why don't we do more tests today on this funny glitch in your ticker and keep you one more night? In the morning, you can go home if you don't have any complaints or pains."

I follow the doctor to the door. "I'm worried about the confusion and the hallucinations," I say softly.

"Losing a life partner is sometimes too difficult for the mind to deal with. Smoke inhalation and oxygen deprivation can also cause confusion."

"This started even before the fire."

He nods. "I'll have the nurses do some discreet cognitive assessments with him while he's still here."

"Thank you."

"Don't worry, yet. Occasional confusion and difficulty remembering doesn't always mean someone is suffering from something like dementia or Alzheimer's. Sometimes, it's just the normal process of the mind slowing down with age. Once, I had a patient whose family was convinced she had dementia. It turns out she'd lost her hearing and didn't want to tell them. She was always confused because she couldn't hear what was being said."

Before he leaves, he runs his hand up and down my arm, reassuring me.

When I return to the room, Sawyer is looking a little jealous.

"Don't worry, I much prefer firefighters to handsome doctors."

"Good choice."

I approach the side of the bed and pause as I pull the covers over my father's fragile-looking body. It looks like he's aged forty years overnight. I mean, he's in his seventies, but until now, I saw him as a strong, handsome man returning from a long day of work and finding the time to play with a feisty, energetic daughter. Seeing him here in this feeble and vulnerable condition is humbling. "Do you hear that, Dad? You might be coming home tomorrow." I frown when he closes his eyes and goes back to sleep. I tidy the room and fold the blanket I used last night.

"Grace."

Sawyer's tortured expression makes me nervous. "Yes?"

"Do you have somewhere to stay?"

I feel all the air leave my lungs as if I've been punched hard in the stomach. A moment of panic follows.

"I'm sorry," he says, reaching for my hand. "I'm sorry to bring it up, but I've been thinking about it all night."

My mind wanders. I know he's still talking, but my only thought now is that I'm homeless. Homeless, and everything is gone. Turned to ash in a pile of smoldering embers. The clothes on my back is all that's left of what I own.

"Grace?" He gently squeezes my hand to bring me back to the current conversation. "You know I have lots of room. You and your father can stay with me. I'd enjoy the company, to be honest."

I can't even comprehend his offer right now. I walk to the side of the bed and hold my father's hand. A strange sound gets my attention. "Do you hear that?" I ask Sawyer. "I heard that same sound inside the house the other day. My dad thought I was crazy."

"It sounds almost like fluttering." He looks around the room for the source. "Grace, look. There's a hummingbird outside the window."

A feeling of angst washes over me, and the hair on the back of my neck stands on end.

Sawyer approaches the window and looks around outside. "The room is very close to the pollinator garden the volunteers plant yearly." He turns to find me completely falling apart. The sound of my hard sobs has him crossing the room in a few enormous strides and pulling me into his arms.

I lean against his muscular chest and tuck myself under his chin, seeking the safety that has always been there for me. The warmth of his body and soothing caress calm me. "Your dad will be in good hands for a few hours while they run tests, so why don't you come home with me for a while? I already stopped and picked up some things you might need, and you need to eat."

I sniffle. "I guess I'll need to buy some clothes."

"Sara has already gathered up some clothes for you. Ben dropped them off at my house. You can freshen up and get some rest before you come back to the hospital for the night." He leans back so he can see my face. "You are coming back to stay with him, right?"

I nod my confirmation as I reach for a tissue.

"Let's get you looked after so you can better look after your dad. Okay?"

I can't answer. I can't even think.

"Grace." He brushes the hair away from my face and brushes away one last tear with the pad of his thumb. "You're not alone through this. I've got you."

Chapter Twelve

When I'm absolutely sure my dad is settled, Sawyer convinces me it's safe to leave him for a short while. I climb into his truck and make the ten-kilometre drive in silence. When he pulls into the long country driveway, I try to wrap my head around the fact that it might be my home for the next little while.

I follow him through the front door and look around at all the boxes and bags in the family room.

Sawyer pauses. "People have been sending stuff over all day. Word spreads fast in this town, and everyone wants to help."

"What is all this?"

"Clothing, toiletries, household items. I have an envelope set aside that's already full of cash donations."

"For us?" I ask, feeling overwhelmed as I follow him up the stairs.

"Mmhmm."

"Why?"

"In case you need anything while you figure it out. I went through the women's clothes and took out some I thought you'd be comfortable in. I washed them and left them on the counter."

"Thank you."

He continues to walk to the end of the hall. "I got the shower working temporarily."

I stare at the clawfoot tub on the other side of the room.

He acknowledges my reaction. "Would you rather have a bath?"

"Tempting. I think I'll have a quick shower and get back to my dad."

"Okay. I'll go make us something to eat."

I don't have any appetite right now, but I know there's no point in arguing with him. I step out of the shower and reach for a towel. The room is cold, and I start to shiver. I grab the pile of clothes and hurry down the hall to the bedroom. It's much warmer in there. He did a great job picking out things I'd wear. I start to dry off, and Sawyer knocks on the door. I'm not sure why I suddenly feel bashful, but I pull the towel around me before I open it.

"Sorry. I forgot to give you these." He hands me a shopping bag containing deodorant, panties, socks...a hairbrush, and a toothbrush—the kind of things nobody would want second hand.

He thinks of everything. "I don't know what to say."

"You don't have to say anything except that you're starving. I made my famous chicken parmesan."

"That sounds fancy."

"Not really. It's shake-and-bake chicken breasts covered in mozzarella cheese, served with spaghetti and canned sauce."

"Mozzarella and not Parmesan?"

"Don't let my secret out of the bag."

"I won't." I hold up the bag of things I need to get ready as a reminder. "I'll be right down."

"Right. Sorry. I'll meet you downstairs."

I sit at the antique dresser and look at myself in the mirror while I brush through my damp hair. I haven't even started to process what happened yet.

I finish getting dressed and join Sawyer in the kitchen. Everything is laid out on the table, and it smells delicious.

"How have you managed to stay single?" I ask perplexed.

He smiles. "I was waiting for the right girl." He hands me a napkin and sits across from me.

I can't remember the last thing I ate. I twirl the spaghetti on my fork, mimicking the way my thoughts are spinning. "Was there anything left?"

Sawyer looks up from his plate.

"At the house. Were you able to save anything?"

"No, Grace. I'm sorry."

I nod my head. "All my school souvenirs and all the pictures of my mom are *gone*."

"I'm afraid so. I stayed in case there was a chance we could have saved anything. There was no hope."

"Thank you for trying." I continue to play with my food. "Do they know yet how it started?"

"I know what you're thinking, and let me assure you there's no reason to believe your dad started it. Preliminary investigation suggests that it was an electrical fire."

"I was afraid that he was trying to cook himself some food while I was working at the shop."

"I know. That's why I'm telling you this. The fire didn't start in the kitchen. There was no evidence of lit candles or burning cigarettes. So far, all the evidence points to bad wiring in an old house."

"I called the insurance company from the hospital last night."

"What did they say?"

"They're going to send out an adjuster. Once the claim is registered, they will call me back with the assessment and the next steps. His policy was fairly outdated. I don't think he ever renewed the value to today's market. At this point, I don't even know if we'll get enough money to rebuild."

"Let's not worry about that today."

"They said they'd cover a hotel for a few days, but if they do approve a rebuild, there's no clause to cover a long-term rental until we can move back in."

"Let's not worry about that today, either. You don't need a hotel. You and your dad can stay here, short-term or long-term."

"It's too much to ask."

"No, it's not. I told you before. Growing up, your dad was like a father to me. There's plenty of room here and several empty bedrooms. Your dad can have the room at the back of the house on the main floor. There are no strings. Let me help, Grace."

"Okay. We'll tell him tonight when we go back."

"Great."

"Sawyer?"

He looks up from his plate again and waits for me to finish my thought.

I try to smile. "If you're done eating, can you drive me back?"

Sawyer takes me by the shop so I can pick up my vehicle, then follows me back to the hospital.

On the way through the lobby, the doctor approaches us. "I was hoping to run into you."

"Is everything okay?" I ask, concerned.

"He's resting quietly, but the tests show anomalies in his heart. They may have always been there, and he didn't know."

"So, what does that mean?"

"Simply put, his heart begins to beat sporadically, and then it takes too long to get back into a normal rhythm. After we had him up and moving around, his oxygen levels were low. We're calling in the best cardiologist for him."

"So, he'll be here a few more days?"

"I think it's possible. It may be easily controlled by medication, but I'll leave it to the cardiologist to decide the best course of action."

"Thank you," Sawyer offers on my behalf.

"I'm not supposed to tell you anything about his medical conditions without his permission. So don't get me in trouble."

"We promise."

The elevator takes forever to get to the top floor. At one point, it stops, and the door opens, but there's no one there. I raise a brow, and Sawyer shrugs before pushing the button to close the doors.

The door opens on the top floor, and I exit into the hallway as if I've been shot out with a slingshot. We pass a rather tall firefighter wearing his gear and covered in soot. "How's it going?" Sawyer stops and asks, intrigued.

He walks past him, steps into the elevator and nods an acknowledgement as the door closes.

"Do you know him?" I ask curiously.

"I've never seen him before. Did that seem really odd to you?"

"It did."

"There was something really odd about what just happened," Sawyer repeats as we reach the room.

I'm pleased to find my dad sitting upright and watching TV. He still looks tired, and the oxygen tubes protruding from his nostrils are a disturbing sight to me.

"How are you feeling, Dad? What did the doctor say about your test results?"

"All these fancy machines, and they still know nothing about nothing," he says, exasperated. "More specialists, more tests, probably more pills."

"Is there anything you need me to bring for you?"

He turns off the television and leans his head back against the pillow. He stares at Sawyer with a weary, pensive expression. "You. Come closer."

Sawyer glances at me with a concerned look before he approaches the side of the bed.

"Are you single, Mr. Kelly?"

"Yes, sir, I am."

"Do you still love my daughter?"

"DAD!" I gasp.

"Stay out of this, Grace." My father warns. "This is a conversation between us men."

My eyes open wide, and I cross my arms in front of me. I avert my attention to Sawyer. "You don't have to answer that."

He doesn't hesitate. "There's a lot to love about your daughter. She's my best friend."

Sawyer locks eyes with mine, and at that moment, I know he's telling the truth. I remind myself to breathe and hold back a strong emotional response.

A peaceful expression washes over my dad's face. "Good. She's made some horrible decisions since you left."

"DAD!"

"Be honest, honey. You've never really given your heart to anyone. It's always been reserved for Sawyer."

Sawyer's eyes glisten, and a ghost of a smile creeps across his lips.

"You look after my daughter," he demands. "Or I'll have that firefighter come back and kick your ass."

"Firefighter?" Sawyer looks in my direction, and I shrug, just as confused.

"What firefighter, Dad?"

"The one that just left. He said he helped your mother pull me out of the fire."

"Oh, boy," I whisper under my breath as the nurse comes in to give him some medication. I ignore the boyish grin Sawyer is giving me from across the room. I'm sure he'll have something to say about my dad's comments. Either that, or he's just going to taunt me silently with the knowledge.

The nurse straightens things on the bedside stand and checks all the monitors and cords. "He told the doctor that he hasn't been sleeping, so he's been prescribed something to help him rest. It will work quickly, so I'd say your goodbyes now."

"I was going to stay with him overnight."

She turns on her heels and walks towards the door. "If anyone asks, I heard nothing, and I know nothing."

My dad's eyes grow heavy, and I pull the chair I previously slept in closer to the side of the bed, preparing for a long night.

"Grace."

"Yes, Dad."

"There's no reason for you to stay."

"I want to be close to you in case you need anything."

"I'll be fine. The nurse's button is attached to my pillow. I'm tired right now."

Torn, I glance over at Sawyer.

He shrugs. "It's up to you. If you're not going to sleep because you're stressed and worried about him, stay. But I think you could use a good night's sleep yourself. You can come back at the crack of dawn if you like. How long do you have off work?"

I purse my lips and close my eyes. "I hadn't even thought about work."

"I'm sure Sara can manage on her own for a few days. If not, Ben and Jake can probably pitch in. You have the insurance people to deal with."

I feel dismayed. "I guess I have things to work out."

"You need to look after yourself first and foremost."

He's right. I won't be any help to my dad if I'm burnt out. I may need to take some time off work and help get him settled.

"Dad, Sawyer has kindly offered to let us stay with him until the house is rebuilt."

"That's very kind. Thank you."

"It's my pleasure."

"Grace, before I forget. My wallet is on the table there. Take it with you. I don't want it to get lost or stolen."

"Got it." I stuff it in my pocket and then reach for my dad's hand as I lean over the bed and place a kiss on his forehead. "Good night, Dad. I'll come back tomorrow."

I nearly fall asleep on the way back to his house, but my head is spinning with everything I need to do. I scribble down notes in a small notebook I carry in my purse.

When we get back to Sawyer's, I sit cross-legged on the couch, trying to decipher my own writing. Sawyer puts a bowl of cat food outside the front door. He shrugs when I give him a knowing smile. "I haven't seen her for a while, but the bowl is always empty."

"The raccoons are probably eating it."

He pauses. "I should check the security footage."

I push a small figurine to the side of the coffee table and put down my notebook.

"That's strange," Sawyer says, scratching his head.

"What?"

"Did you put that there?"

I look over at the small porcelain figurine of a lady sitting on what looks like a garden bench. "No. It was there when I came in."

Sawyer picks it up and walks across the room. "It was in this cabinet." He twists the key in the antique lock and springs open the fragile glass door. After placing it where it belongs, he secures the door again and gives me a confused look. "Come to think of it. That's not the first thing I've found in a different place lately."

"Well, maybe it's your aunt…" I pause and wait for him to fill in the blank.

"Vera."

"Maybe Aunt Vera is trying to make me feel at home."

"What do you mean?"

"There was creepy stuff going on at my house, remember?"

"Did you extend the invitation to your homeless ghosts?"

"Why would you say that aloud? Don't even put stuff like that out into the universe."

He holds his hand up in the air. "Sorry! I was just joking around."

"There is nothing funny about...*ghosts*," I whisper the last word.

"How are things going?" he asks, looking at my notebook. "What can I help with?"

"Nothing. I've got it under control."

"Sara, Ben, Jake, and I can take some things off your plate and help lighten the load."

"Thanks, but I'm good."

He sighs heavily. "I'm not taking on this argument tonight. It's late. Up to bed with you if we're heading back to the hospital early."

I drop my feet to the floor and stand, not sure I have enough energy to walk myself up the stairs. Sawyer reaches for my hand when we get to the top of the staircase. I pause.

"Will you stay in my room with me tonight?"

I hesitate. I hadn't given any thought to where I would sleep.

"Please. I promise no hanky panky. I just want to be close to you tonight."

I'm not going to lie. I sleep better when he's beside me. Maybe tonight I'll get some sleep.

"Okay. I'll go brush my teeth and get changed."

When I open his bedroom door, he's already in bed. He lifts the blankets to welcome me in, and I notice he's wearing pyjama pants that say, *'I never dreamed I'd grow up to be a super cool park ranger, but here I am, absolutely killing it.'* I laugh as I climb in beside him. He lifts his arm, and I snuggle in, fitting perfectly against his bare chest. He presses his lips against my forehead. "Good night."

I yawn as I start to wish him goodnight, too. I'm not sure I finish the words before I drift off to sleep.

Chapter Thirteen

My alarm springs to life, startling me awake. I'd be okay if I never heard another siren or alarm for the rest of my life. Sawyer is dressed and waiting to take me back to see my dad. He has breakfast laid out on the table ready.

"Did you sleep well?" he asks as he clears the plates off the table.

"I think so. I don't remember waking up at all."

He smirks, and I become suspicious. "What?"

"You snore."

"I do not."

"Yup. You snore. And you drool."

I roll my eyes. "That's really immature of you to mention it."

"It was cute as fuck. I always wondered."

"There's something wrong with you."

Sawyer grins.

I try to massage the stiffness out of my neck as we walk to the truck. "I really hope they'll let him go home today. I feel like all we do is drive back and forth from the house to the hospital."

As we pull out onto the highway, he's still amused by our morning conversation. "Tell me honestly. All the time we spent together...even though it was just as friends, weren't there things you wondered about?"

I think about it for a minute. "Well, yes, there was one thing."

"What?"

"I noticed you have very small feet for a man."

He raises his brow and glances at me. "Well, now you know for sure that's just a myth."

I smile, pleased with myself. "Yes, it definitely is a myth."

We hold hands as we walk through the parking lot and into the lobby of the small-town hospital. Sawyer buys me tea before we head upstairs. There are only a few floors, but the elevator is painfully slow in responding. When we finally get in and press the button, Sawyer leans against the wall and crosses his leg at the ankle. Having him back in my life is both exhilarating and terrifying. I think a lot about what my dad said. Is it possible my heart was never wholly open for anybody else? Maybe I did reserve it for Sawyer all this time.

"Kiss me."

I blink rapidly, stunned at the suggestion. "What?"

His slow advance forces me to retreat until I can go no further. His last stride is long and quick, pinning me where I stand. I try not to spill my tea as the elevator stops at our floor and the doors slide open. Sawyer curses.

I laugh as we exit the elevator, amused at the timing. The ordinarily quiet floor is full of people rushing back and forth. I stop dead in the middle of the hall, getting a very bad vibe. Sawyer's brow creases in concern as Doctor Fulton runs directly into my dad's room from the nurse's station. I drop my cup and run to the doorway. Several nurses and Doctor Fulton stand in a circle around his bed. Bells and whistles and sirens are screeching, and everyone is yelling instructions. I try to move further into the room, but Sawyer holds me firm. "Stay out of the way and let them do their thing!" Suddenly, everyone stops and stares as the room grows eerily quiet except for the single-note tone. Adrenaline overcomes me, and I break free of Sawyer's hold. They look at me sympathetically as I frantically scream. "Why are you just standing there? Do something!"

"Grace, we can't," Grant says apologetically.

"What do you mean you can't? You're a doctor! Bring him back. BRING HIM BACK!"

A nurse tries to settle me and moves me away from the bedside. "He signed a DNR," she informs me.

I glance at Sawyer, confused. "He signed a do not resuscitate order?"

Grant nods. "Yes. Last night. We strongly suggested he wait to talk it over with you, but he asked us not to discuss it with you."

"NO!" I scream. "NO, NO, NO, NO!"

"I'm sorry, but we're bound by law."

Sawyer muscles past everyone at the bedside. "I'm not," he informs the doctor as he begins efforts to bring my father back to life. I fight the nurse who's preventing me from reaching the bedside until she finally releases me.

"What do I do?" I ask Sawyer hysterically. "How do I help?" A few minutes pass, but Sawyer's attempts are unsuccessful. Grant stands behind him and places a firm hand on his shoulder, giving it an empathetic squeeze. With tears in his eyes, Sawyer establishes eye contact with me. "I'm so sorry, Grace. He's gone."

I place my hand over my mouth as I lower my head and begin to cry.

"Take a moment and say goodbye," Doctor Fulton says.

I reach for my father's hand and squeeze it; I'm guessing to test the truth of the situation. I close my eyes as my chin begins to quiver. I can't believe it. I just can't believe he's gone. It can't be happening. Sawyer takes me in his arms and then guides me out of the room and out of the way of the hospital staff so they can do whatever they do when someone passes in their care. My attention is drawn to a middle-aged woman wearing a white nightgown standing in the doorway across the hall. Her eyes are glassy, and her features are tired and frail. "He is free now," she assures me. An orderly quickly ushers her back into her room, but it unnerves me. As I walk with Sawyer down the hallway, I look over my shoulder to find her peeking around the door at us.

A janitor places a caution sign over the wet floor where he's just cleaned up the tea I abandoned when I saw the commotion. The lights in the elevator flick on and off, and it stops on every floor, but no one is waiting when the doors open. Sawyer tries to hide his expression, but I can tell he's as spooked as I am.

Memories of my mother's passing come rushing back to me as we walk through the cold and sterile lobby. I know some things need to be done, but I don't know where to start. I don't know how I'm going to get through it. My legs begin to feel weak. "I need to sit down."

Sawyer directs me to a row of seats against the wall as a distinguished gentleman in a black suit approaches us. "Grace?"

My brow furrows. "Yes?"

"I'm from the funeral home."

I sit up straight. "Wow, that's fast. Do you sit around the corner waiting for news of someone passing on your CB radio?"

"My deepest sympathies. The hospital called us."

"Oh, so you're on speed dial," I say sarcastically. "How does that work? Is it like a taxi at the airport? You all wait in line for the next body?"

"Grace," Sawyer says, trying to calm me.

"I met with your father a few days ago. He called us to make some pre-arrangements."

My chest becomes tight, and I struggle to breathe. I know he's still talking, but all I hear is an echoing in my head.

"Grace! Are you okay?" Sawyer asks, holding on to me. "It looks like you're going to pass out."

"He knew."

Sawyer squints. "He knew what?"

"He knew he was going to die."

The funeral director sits beside me, holding a tissue. "Not necessarily. Sometimes, when a person has been through a traumatic event, such as a fire, they become aware of how fragile life is and feel a sense of urgency to get things in order.”

I turn and lock eyes with Sawyer. “HE KNEW.”

He purses his lips, though he doesn’t want to disagree. “Maybe.”

The funeral director gets to his feet. “We’ve come to take him to the funeral home, but there’s no reason for you to do anything tonight. Give us a call tomorrow and let us know when you can come in to discuss the arrangements.”

“Wait! You’re taking him already?”

“My co-worker was arranging the transport while I came to find you. I’m certain they’re already gone.”

I turn my head and give Sawyer a pleading look as if I expect there is something he can do. He returns my sorrowful expression. “Grace, let’s go home and get some rest, and I’ll take you to see him tomorrow.”

“I’m so sorry for your loss,” the funeral director says before he walks away, leaving me dumbfounded in the middle of the foyer.

I have no words on the way home. I have no thoughts. I have no feeling. I’m completely numb. When my mom passed, I cried. I cried until I physically couldn’t cry any longer. My very soul has become a desert, void of precipitation. Perhaps I’ve already reached the brink of emotional thresholds, and my brain has switched to survival mode. Sawyer glances at me several times during the drive, monitoring my strife and preparing to provide support.

"I just want to go to bed," I say as we enter the dark foyer of the century home. "Alone."

Sawyer nods. "Okay, Grace. Whatever makes you comfortable. Do you need anything?"

I walk away without answering. There is a heavier, ominous feeling in the house tonight. I climb into the spare bed, fully clothed, and turn off the bedside lamp. Sleep comes swiftly, and I am almost lost in the comforting protection of the dream realm when I hear the floor creak in a cadence that would suggest footsteps. I'm semi-conscious when I experience the distinct feeling of the blankets tightening around my legs as if someone has just sat on the side of the bed. When I open my eyes and see my mother sitting there, I gasp and sit upright. All fear leaves my body as the ghostly manifestation turns to me with the comforting smile I haven't seen in quite some time. I blink my eyes rapidly, trying to focus in the darkness. Eager to affirm her visit, I reach to turn on the bedside lamp to light the room, but she fades away before my very eyes.

The door opens, and Sawyer whispers my name. "Grace? Are you okay?"

I hesitate too long to answer, so he enters the room to check for himself. A tear trails down my cheek as I struggle with the decision to share my experience just now. We were half joking about it earlier, but I don't know if Sawyer actually believes in ghosts. I'm not even sure if I do. Perhaps it was wishful thinking or my mind manifesting a much-needed coping mechanism.

"Bad dream?" he asks, concerned.

Stunned by the sight of him standing in the room bare-chested and with nothing on but his boxers, I nod.

"I'll stay if you want."

Acting without thinking for a change, I move over so he can crawl in beside me. He tugs the blanket over us and pulls me tight against his body, holding me firmly until exhaustion wins and I surrender.

It feels like it's only been moments, but I wake long after sunrise to the feeling of being completely wrapped in a blanket of muscle. I turn in his arms, forcing him to adjust his position as I seek out more warmth against his chest. The gentle rhythm of his breathing soothes me. I feel at peace. Sawyer has a way of making me feel like I can let my guard down. He makes me believe I'm safe enough to have moments of vulnerability without feeling weak or powerless.

As the walls come down, the events of the past few days come flooding back to my conscious mind, causing strong emotions to build within me.

Now, fully awake and aware, Sawyer holds my gaze, locked in a tender moment. Stroking my hair, he brushes it away from my face. As he moves in closer, I eagerly meet his kiss, opening my lips and slipping my warm tongue inside. Sawyer is the guy whose kiss will set the standard by which all other kisses will be judged for the rest of my life. Because it's not just a kiss; it's a level of connection I have never experienced with anyone else.

"I have always loved you," he whispers as he shifts his muscular body to make me more comfortable. I release a heavy sigh as I lay my head against his chest. The words are on the tip of my tongue, but before I can say them, a loud voice echoes through the house. My brow raises.

"It's Jake. I'll go see what he needs."

"I'm going to have a quick shower."

Sawyer takes a robe off a hook on the back of the door and holds it open for me to put on.

"That's a tad old-fashioned," I comment aloud.

He shrugs. "Maybe, but this house is cold." He cinches the tie around my waist and then laughs at how big it is on me. "Be careful you don't fall."

"I'm not worried. If I do, this thing will break my fall."

He chuckles. "I suspect it would be the equivalent of dropping on a gym mat." He opens the bedroom door. "I'll be right down," he hollers to Jake as he heads towards the stairs.

"You might want to put some pants on first."

"Good idea," he says as he changes direction and goes to his room first.

It's taking some coercion to get the shower working this morning. I have to twist and turn and curse at the faucet before I finally get a steady flow of water. But even the soothing flow of warm water can't wash away all the tragic events of the past few days.

I get dressed and join the guys downstairs.

"I'm so sorry for your loss," Jake says as I enter the room.

"Thank you. It was a shock. We expected him to come home in a day or two."

Sawyer wraps his arms around me from behind.

"I wish there was something I can say. Sorry, just doesn't seem enough." He looks down at something he's clutching in his hands. "I brought you this."

He hands me a suit, and I narrow my eyes, confused.

"It's an old suit of my father's. He sent it over. He thought you might need it to bury your dad since everything he owned would have been lost in the fire."

Speechless, I clutch the garment tightly.

"You don't have to use it. We won't be offended if you'd rather buy something new."

Sawyer squeezes my shoulder. "Grace?"

I shake my head, trying to snap myself out of a haze. "It's perfect and very much appreciated. Thank you."

"I'm going to get out of your hair so you can take that to the funeral home." He stretches his hand out to Sawyer. "When you're ready to get at these projects, just let us know."

Sawyer closes the door behind him and takes my hands. "We don't have to rush over there. We can go whenever you're ready."

"I'm ready."

"Breakfast first?"

"I don't think I can eat right now."

He frowns. "Me neither."

Sawyer parks his truck out front of the funeral home on the main street of town. I sit in silence, looking at my hands in my lap. Sawyer watches and patiently waits.

"Do you want me to go in and tell them you need a minute? Or we can reschedule for later."

"Sounds like there's nothing much for me to do besides pick a date."

"As upset as you are about that, trust me, he did you a favour. Now, you don't have to guess what he would have wanted. He already made those arrangements."

I swallow hard and get out of the truck. One of the employees respectfully holds open the door. We're greeted by several people standing in the hallway, all sharing their condolences. At the end of the hall a distinguished looking man, in a black suit, extends his hand. "We have him ready in the parlour if you'd like a few moments alone."

I squeeze Sawyer's hand tightly, trying to muster the courage to walk into the room.

"When you're ready, you can meet me in the office and go over the details."

I take one step and stop. Sawyer gives my hand a reassuring squeeze. At the far side of the dimly lit parlour, there's a coffin, and I summon all the strength I have to put one foot in front of the other to cross the room.

"It doesn't look like him," I sniffle.

"I don't think they ever look like themselves once their life force has left them."

"I can't believe this is real." Tears well in my eyes. "I keep thinking I'm going to wake up, and it's all a bad dream."

"I know." Holding me tightly against his chest, Sawyer does his best to console me.

Chapter Fourteen

My dad didn't want much fuss. There was a closed casket visitation for an hour at the funeral home. There were no speeches, no words of recollection or reflection on his life by me or anyone else. It was a brief, humble goodbye. That's the way he wanted it.

In keeping with the tone of my life thus far, there are torrential downpours as we make our way to the cemetery. The sky is dark and angry, and so am I.

"Sara has some food to drop off at the house afterwards," Sawyer says as he navigates the car through the century-old stone pillars at the cemetery's gates.

"Okay."

"I know your dad didn't want a big fuss or anything at the funeral, but what do you want? Would you find comfort in having friends come back to the house?"

I hadn't really thought about my needs. I shrug. "I don't know."

He gives me a sympathetic smile. "If you're up to it, feel free to invite people back to the house for a coffee and snacks."

"What about something stronger?" I ask as we come to the end of the dirt path and can't drive any further.

"Whatever you need. I've got you." Sawyer assures me.

Sawyer's friends are already out of their cars and ensuring everyone in attendance makes it to the graveside safely. At the grave, the oversized tombstone marks the place where my parents will rest together for eternity. In preparation for this day, my dad had his name inscribed beside my mother's when she passed, leaving room for the dates to be filled in when it was time. I've seen it every time I've come to visit my mom, but today, it hits me like a hammer in the chest. Despite Sawyer standing with an oversized umbrella over me, the harsh, driving rain hits me in the face relentlessly. After a few short words are spoken by a non-denominational officiant at the grave, I feel cold and numb.

The ground is muddy and slippery. Not ideal conditions for a burial on the side of a hill in one of the area's oldest country cemeteries. Sawyer has a firm grip on my elbow on the way to the car. In my foggy state, I hear my name. I look around as I walk, but there's no one left behind. Everyone has made a quick retreat to their vehicles to get out of the miserable elements. Sawyer opens the passenger door to my car and holds it for me. I pause and take one last look around the cemetery and notice an elderly woman with silver hair watching from a distance. She feels familiar to me, but I don't recall her being at the service at the funeral home.

Sawyer looks over his shoulder, curious about what I'm looking at. "Someone you know?"

"I'm not sure."

"Get in. You're shivering." He cranks the heat as soon as he starts the car.

When I glance back toward the hill no one is there.

All the way back to the house, I think about how strange it feels to know I'll never see my dad again. The rain doesn't let up, forcing us to dash quickly to the door. No matter how hard we try, it's impossible to avoid the flooded walkways and ankle-deep puddles. The small calico cat has found a safe, dry spot in the front garden, protected by the trees and the overhang of the roof. I stand at the door and try to coax her into the house, but she's content where she is.

I'm about to close the door behind me when I see Sara pull in. I wait at the door as Sara rushes through the swamp with Maya following close behind.

"It's raining cats and dogs," she says, exasperated.

"Apparently, it only rains cats at this farm," I joke. The house is cold and damp. "Come in," I say, stepping to the side. "Sawyer is getting a fire going, so it will warm up quickly. Let me take that." I reach for some of the containers they are juggling while trying to kick off their wet shoes.

Sawyer meets us on the way to the kitchen. "What can I help with?"

"Nothing. We've got it."

"Is this all for us?" I'm overwhelmed as I look around and notice there's not one empty space on the counter.

"Well, people usually send flowers with their condolences, but since your dad didn't want any, people sent food instead."

"Much more practical," Sawyer admits.

"I hope you have a freezer," Maya says, moving some of the containers around.

"Hello?" a voice hollers from the front foyer.

"In the kitchen," Sawyer calls out.

"What smells so good?" Ben asks as he joins us.

"Lasagna, meatloaf, chilli, macaroni and cheese—you name it, we've got it."

"I know where I'm eating dinner all week," Jake says, sneaking in.

"Where'd you come from?" I ask, startled.

"I let myself in. On my way past, I threw some more wood on the fire. It looked like it was going out."

"Thanks. I turned the heat on, but the oil furnace is old, and it takes a long time to kick in."

"That should be on our list of upgrades," Ben notes. "I'm shocked the roof doesn't leak."

"Don't even put that out into the universe," Sawyer says as he looks nervously at the ceiling.

"I brought donuts and coffee. I left them in the other room," Jake says, walking out of the kitchen. Everyone follows, eager to warm their feet by the fire.

"Where's your father?" I ask Jake as I warm my hands on the paper takeaway cup.

"He was tired, so I dropped him off at home."

"Is he okay?"

"He's lost too many old friends lately. I think it's starting to weigh heavy on his mind."

I frown. "Make sure you cherish every moment you have with him. Take nothing for granted. Not one single minute."

"Message received, loud and clear."

"Grace, is there anything you need?" Maya asks, concerned.

"No, I'm good. Sawyer bought anything and everything a person could possibly need. Sara made sure I'm not wandering around naked."

"Goodness. We couldn't have that!" Sara exclaims.

"There's no point in collecting housewares or furniture until I have details about rebuilding from the insurance company."

Sawyer stuffs the last bite of a chocolate donut into his mouth. "I'm hoping she'll decide she can't live without me and stay here with me."

I give him a half smile. I wouldn't say I'm against the idea, but it's too soon to make any decisions. I learned in psychology classes that sometimes traumatic situations can fast-forward relationships, pushing them past the very important steps of discovery. In those very fragile situations, emotional needs can become the foundation of the relationship instead of a healthy mutual trust and respect.

The boys start talking about Sawyer's plans for the property. Sara has a few ideas of her own. I notice Maya becomes a bit flustered, and I glance curiously at what she's staring at in the far corner of the room. She nervously establishes eye contact with me and then rejoins the conversation. Now she has me spooked, and I keep looking at the cabinet in the corner.

I yawn, and the room goes quiet. "We should get going," Ben says, getting to his feet. Everyone follows him into the foyer, and I stand out of the way at the entrance to the room. One by one, they say their goodbyes. Maya stands near me, waiting for the gridlock at the door to clear. She slips her shoes on very slowly, looking like there's something she wants to say.

She takes a few steps toward the door and then stops to look at the framed family pictures hanging on the wall. It feels to me like she's stalling. Sawyer joins us and stands behind me with his arms wrapped around my middle. "Who is this lady?" Maya asks, pointing at one of the pictures.

"That's my Aunt Vera."

"Did she die in this house?" Maya asks while studying the picture carefully.

"She was born, and she died in this house."

Maya relaxes a little and smiles. "She was quite a character."

Sawyer releases me and then moves toward the picture. "She really was."

He scratches his head, curious about Maya's strange behaviour. "I better go keep an eye on the fire. Thanks for everything. We should all get together soon under different circumstances."

He leaves me standing in the hall alone with her. I walk toward the door and pull it open. Maya smiles and hands me a small slip of paper. "This is my cell number. If you need anything, please don't hesitate to call."

"Thank you, again." I take the paper out of her hand, and she holds it so I can't pull it away.

Leaning in, she whispers in my ear. "She's having some fun with you two, but she's harmless. Don't let her scare you away."

A sudden chill moves through the entranceway, and I'm feeling a little unnerved. She stands straight and zips up her coat, then establishes eye contact.

"Do you understand what I'm talking about?"

I nod. "I do."

"Does Sawyer?"

"I don't think so."

"Well, he is a man. There's a logical explanation for everything."

I'm shocked, and I have so many questions. "So you…"

"Apparently."

"Do they…"

"Sometimes."

"Can you…"

"No."

"Are my…"

"I'm afraid not."

I stand with a blank expression, not sure what to say next.

"I'm happy you have Sawyer. Lean on him. He won't let you down."

She leaves me standing at the door, trying to gather my thoughts. I'm not sure what just happened. I walk into the kitchen to make sure everything has been put away. As I tidy the counter, my attention is drawn to the side of the refrigerator. A cold chill runs through me. "Sawyer!" I yell loudly.

He rushes into the room. "What's wrong?"

"I thought you said you weren't able to salvage anything from the fire?"

"I wasn't. There was nothing left to save."

I pace back and forth in the small space, mumbling.

"Grace, what's wrong?"

I point at the side of the fridge. "That!"

He moves beside me, and I feel his body stiffen. "Where did those come from?" he asks, looking at the fridge magnets from destinations around the world.

"You didn't put them there?"

"No. I've never seen them before. What's going on?"

I hold my hand on my heart. "These are the exact same magnets my parents collected when they used to travel. These are all the places we went on family vacations."

"I don't understand. I don't think Aunt Vera did any travelling."

He acknowledges my expression of fear. "Grace? What are you thinking?"

"These are the magnets off my parent's fridge. These are from my house."

"That doesn't make any sense. How would they have gotten here?"

"I don't know. I can't answer that."

He reaches for me and tugs me into his arms. "There has to be some reasonable explanation."

"Any explanation would be welcome."

166

“If it’s that upsetting, I’ll get rid of them.”

“No!”

“What do you want me to do with them then?”

“Just leave them where they are. They’re there for a reason. I don’t know if someone is trying to send me a message or if the house is giving me a gift. It all seems crazy to me right now.”

He leads me into the other room and settles on the couch in front of the fire. “I bet I know what happened. Somebody must have brought them tonight, thinking they’d remind you of your dad and bring you comfort. They can’t be the exact ones from the house; they would have been destroyed like everything else. In the morning, I’ll text everyone and see who left them there.”

That explanation calms me a bit. It sounds almost logical. He holds me protectively in his arms. “Do you need anything?”

“No, I’m fine. The fire is making me sleepy.”

“Lucky you. I shouldn’t have drank coffee this late. I’m sure I’ll be up all night.”

“Well, if you get hungry, there’s lots to eat,” I giggle.

“I’m sorry, Grace.”

“For what?”

“For everyone just showing up here.”

“Oh. I didn’t mind. It was kind of nice to have people in the house. It made it feel like...”

“Home?”

“Home.”

He squeezes me tighter. "It makes me really happy to hear that."

I take a long, slow breath. "My dad would have loved it here."

Sawyer kisses my forehead, and we spend a few moments in silence as the fire begins to burn down.

"So," Sawyer begins. "I've only met Maya a few times at Sara's. She's a little different, don't you think?"

"She seems nice," I say, trying to stay clear of where I suspect this conversation is going.

"Yes, she's definitely nice, but something about her seemed a little *off* tonight. Did you notice?"

"No, I didn't but then I'm so tired I don't think I'm very observant at the moment."

"So, you didn't think her comment about my aunt was a little odd?"

I smile. "I did, actually. But she's certainly not the strangest person to cross my path recently."

"No?"

"No, there's this guy that walks around the house wearing park ranger pyjama pants."

"Oh, I know him. He's a great guy."

"You think so? I'd say he's a little weird."

Sawyer leans so he can see my face. "Weird?"

I laugh as I get to my feet and fold the blanket.

"Oh, I see how it is." He stands and extinguishes what's left of the fire. "Your new friend can see dead people, and I'm the weird one."

"You picked up on that, did you?"

"I know I'm a man," he scoffs. "But I'm not totally blind."

I begin to walk up the stairs.

"And," he continues as he follows me, "since you don't like my park ranger pyjama pants, I'm not going to wear any to bed tonight."

I turn to look at him with my brows raised. "Oh, no. This is not a pyjama-optional relationship. What would your aunt think?"

"I don't really care," he says as he stomps like a child into the bedroom and drops his pants to the floor.

It's hard not to laugh. "You keep that thing covered up. I don't want it touching me in the middle of the night."

Sawyer defiantly climbs into bed stark naked. I wrap one of the blankets around me, creating a barrier. Sawyer chuckles, then rolls over and kisses me goodnight.

"Sawyer?"

"Yes?"

"Thank you. I don't think I could have made it through this day without you."

"You're wrong. You're the strongest woman I know. You would have gotten through it, but I'm glad I was here for you."

Chapter Fifteen

I'm awake at the crack of dawn. I lay there for what seemed like hours, unable to go back to sleep before deciding to go down to the kitchen and rummage through the cupboards. Overripe bananas on the table give me an idea, and by the time Sawyer wakes and follows his nose downstairs, I'm taking freshly baked banana bread out of the oven.

"Why did you let me sleep so late?"

"I figured you needed it. I know your new job was good enough to give you a few days off, but you'll be back in training again soon."

He leans over and kisses me, but it's just a distraction to steal another piece of banana bread.

"You could have just asked for another piece."

"Where's the fun in that?"

"What are you doing?" I ask as he practically upturns the contents of one of the drawers.

"Ben has already texted me this morning that he wants the measurements of the window in the library. He thinks Jake has one in the barn around the same era that will fit."

"Library?"

"Well, I guess it was the office or study because that's where the desk is where she sat to pay the bills. I call it the library because that's where all the books are, and I pay all my bills online."

"This house is so huge I haven't seen all the rooms yet."

"Ah," he says, delighted. "Follow me. You're in for a treat."

I follow him down a narrow hallway decorated with wainscoting wall panels and crown moulding. When we enter the grand room with the ornate trim and built-in bookshelves, I gasp.

"Beautiful, right?" he says proudly.

"It is."

I skim the books as Sawyer takes the window measurements.

"You're not going to believe this."

Sawyer turns to look. "What?"

I pull a book off the shelf and walk toward him with it. "Look familiar?" I ask as I hold it in front of him.

"Wow, that must have been a popular romance book in its day."

I thumb through the pages.

"You're not going to tell me you think that's the book from your house, are you?"

"No. But all the same pages are turned down," I chuckle.

"Look at you, Aunt Vera. Good for you! Maybe we should look at those dog-eared pages later."

"Maybe," I say, smiling as I place it on the desk. Sawyer writes numbers on his notepad, and suddenly, he narrows his eyes.

"What's the matter?" I ask.

"Who is that?"

"Where?"

I turn and look around the room, and Sawyer gives me a strange look. "Outside, coming up the driveway. Who did you think was in here?"

I shrug as I lean to look around the bushes. "Someone riding a bike? Is it one of your neighbours?"

"I don't think so. That's a really old bike. I don't know anyone who would ride a bike like that on these roads. The neighbours would have hopped on an A.T.V."

As the woman nears the front walkway, she stops and gets off her bike, and as she puts out the kickstand, I recognize her as the woman from the hospital the day my dad died.

Sawyer follows me through the house and out the front door.

"Good morning!" she says cheerfully.

"Good morning. Can we help you?" Sawyer asks suspiciously.

"I'm sorry to bother you today. I was in the hospital on the same floor as your father."

I suddenly remember. "And you were at the cemetery yesterday."

"Yes, that was me. I know this is a bad time since he just passed, and you're still mourning."

"Do you think?" Sawyer interrupts, feeling annoyed.

"It's okay, Sawyer." I walk the garden pathway toward her. "What can I help you with?"

"I was wondering if we could have a wee chat. Maybe a cup of tea?"

For some reason, I'm drawn to this woman, and despite Sawyer's censure, I agree. "How about right now?"

"Grace!" Sawyer says, concerned.

I wave him off. "Have you got any other plans right now?"

"No, I don't have any plans."

"And you've ridden your bicycle all the way out here from town?" Sawyer asks, giving me a warning look.

"Yes, but I love to ride, and it's a beautiful day after all that rain."

"Could you excuse us for a minute? I need to talk to Grace."

"Of course." She looks down to find the calico kitten rubbing against her leg. She smiles and bends over to scratch behind her ears.

Sawyer pulls me by the arm behind a nearby bush and out of sight.

"What is wrong with you?" I ask, annoyed at his persistence.

"Are you crazy?" he asks irritably. "You know nothing about this lady. She could have been in the hospital for a psych evaluation."

"I highly doubt it. They keep those people locked up securely on a different floor."

He mutters under his breath.

"There was something in her eyes the night he died. She said he was finally free."

"What does that mean?"

"I don't know. I guess we'll find out while we drink our tea."

"I have a feeling this is a bad idea."

"Look. Even the cat is comfortable with her. You're overreacting."

I step back onto the path and into her view. "Let's step inside for tea."

"I'll put the kettle on," Sawyer says begrudgingly.

"He makes excellent tea," I assure her as we enter through the front door.

"There's a wonderful aura in this house," she says as she follows me to the kitchen. "But it's full of people."

I lower a brow.

"I don't mean the living kind. Some of them followed you here."

"That would explain a lot," I mumble under my breath. Sawyer was right. This just got weird.

"Let me know when the kettle is boiled, dear. I'll make the tea."

"It's okay. I've got this," Sawyer assures her.

"I insist. It's a loose tea leaf I need to use."

"Use for what?" I ask curiously.

"To read your tea leaves."

Sawyer cocks his head to the side and then shakes it quickly. "I'll be outside if you need me."

When the kettle starts to whistle, she takes a small paper bag out of her purse, dumps loose leaves in the bottom of a teacup, and pours the boiling water in. I look into the cup that she slides in front of me. "How do you drink it without getting the stuff in your mouth?"

"You sip it. Have you ever had your tea leaves read?"

"No, I haven't.

"Drink that down, and when you get to the bottom, we'll see what message it has for us."

I try to sip the hot tea without scalding my tongue. It cools off rather quickly in this drafty house, but it's virtually impossible to drink without getting tea leaves in my mouth.

"Before your father left this world, he had a message for you. He wanted you to know that it was time for him to join your mother."

"Are you saying that he wanted to die?" I pass her my cup, unable to drink any more liquid from the saturated tea leaves.

"I'm saying he was *ready*. He doesn't want you to let anything hold you back." She reaches for my hand. "Hold on to love as hard as you can."

"And he told you this, when?"

"Turn your cup upside down on the saucer."

I comply, waiting for her to answer my question.

"Now turn it back up so we can see what's left inside."

She leans over and stares into the bottom of the cup. Curious, I lean in to see what she's looking at. I'm beginning to feel like I'm a victim of a hoax.

"That makes sense," she says with a knowing expression.

All I see is a clump of wet tea leaves. "What makes sense?"

"Do you see the hummingbird in your tea leaves?"

I squint. "Okay, if you say so." I look at it again, straining to see what she sees.

"It's clear."

"Maybe to you," I say, growing impatient and wishing I had listened to Sawyer.

"When you see it, you'll know."

"See what?"

"The sign. It's the confirmation you're looking for. Hope. The end of the journey. A new light." She takes a dramatic pause. "Watch for the shimmer. It's a rare occurrence. When you witness it, you will know it's a sign."

I sit perfectly still, but my eyes dart around the room, looking for whatever she might be talking about.

She laughs. "I don't think it will happen right now, dear."

Sawyer pokes his head into the room. "Everything okay in here?"

I shrug. "I guess so."

"You've been very kind to let me have tea with you today. I'll get going now and leave you to start healing."

She closes the door behind her, and Sawyer looks at me, confused. "Wait. Did she have an Irish accent when she got here? I could swear she just spoke with an Irish accent."

"It wouldn't surprise me. The past several days have been all kinds of weird."

I watch for her out the window. "Where did she go?"

"I have no idea. But I'll tell you this…I walked down to the road to check the mailbox, and our road is a mud bog. There is no way a woman her age cycled that old bike without all-terrain wheels for more than a kilometre from the highway in the mud. And it's eight kilometres from town."

"I admit that seems like an impossible task."

"Did you ask her how she knew where you were staying? How did she find us out here?"

My eyes open wide, and I get the wiggins. "I don't have any explanation for that."

He picks up the teacup and saucer and walks to the sink before pausing. "Can I dump this out? Or will something tragic happen to me?" he jests.

"Your guess is as good as mine. Do you see a hummingbird in that mess of tea leaves?"

Sawyer holds the cup at different angles to reflect the light. "I do not."

I shrug. "Me neither, but apparently, it's there."

After dinner Sawyer draws me a warm bath while I pour myself a massive glass of wine. "I bought you your own robe. It's hanging on the back of the door," he says as I enter the room. He looks at the size of my wine glass and gives me a strong expression of disapproval. "Don't lock the door just in case you fall asleep in there."

"Are you a lifeguard now?"

"Just a concerned boyfriend."

I pause and think about a smartass comeback but decide he's being sincere.

His voice becomes rough and demanding. "If you're not out in half an hour, I'm coming in." He closes the door behind him. I'm not usually into bossy men, but I don't mind Sawyer's authoritative commands. It's kind of hot when he gets dominant in a protective kind of way.

I'm glad to be free of the restrictive clothes I chose for the funeral, and I sigh as I lower myself into the soothing hot water. Sawyer was right to be concerned. The emotional and physical exhaustion, the wine and the heat of the tub hit me hard and hit me fast. I close my eyes, dangerously close to falling asleep. I hear a click, and what sounds to me like the doorknob turning. I open my eyes and watch it closely, trying to detect movement.

I have no idea how long I've been soaking, but an unsettling feeling has me getting to my feet and grabbing the robe from the back of the door. "Sawyer?" I say softly.

I steady myself a moment, feeling a little lightheaded. When there's no response, I pull the robe around me and step into the hall. "Sawyer?" I say louder.

"Do you need something?" he calls from the bottom of the stairs. I look at the doorknob and the distance to the staircase. "No. I'm going to come down and watch T.V."

I dry my hair and put on my pyjamas. Feeling self-conscious, I tug my robe around me and tighten the tie.

Sawyer takes the empty glass out of my hand. "Do you want a refill?"

"The answer to that question is always…yes."

I plop down on the couch and pick up the remote. Sawyer returns with a fresh glass of wine and places it on the coffee table. Then, he goes to the other room to call Ben and plan the next phase of the house restoration. There's nothing on television that interests me—not that it matters because I'm not paying attention anyway. The wine did a good job of relaxing me. Even with the strange and eerie things around me, I close my eyes and fall asleep.

The last thing I remember is putting on my pyjamas and watching T.V. on the couch. When I open my eyes, Sawyer is carrying me into the bedroom. I have no idea how he managed to get me upstairs. With strong biceps, he lowers me onto the bed as if I were a small child and pulls the blanket over me. "Good night," he whispers before kissing me on the head and climbing in beside me.

Probably the worst decision of my life was taking psychology as a minor in college. Now, with a little education, I can overthink *everything*. I never seem to solve my own problems. Just make them worse. While I lay awake, I overanalyze everything. I'd been holding on to the idea that Sawyer was the key to my happiness, and seeing him again gave me hope. But I'm cursed by tragic loss and doomed to live a heartbreaking existence. These things weren't supposed to continue to happen when Sawyer came back. Maybe he's not the key after all.

Chapter Sixteen

I wake up several times during the night, tossing and turning restlessly. Strange sounds and bad dreams thwart my hopes of a good night's sleep.

When the sun begins to rise, and I can see daylight through the window, I give up all hope of sleep, drag myself downstairs, and flop on the couch. Not long after, I hear Sawyer humming in the kitchen and the clatter of dishes.

Every reflection in the room has me on edge. Sawyer places a cup of tea in front of me and sits. "Do you want to talk about it?"

"What?"

"Whatever kept you awake all night."

"There's not much to tell."

"Was it something that lady said?"

"You mean the mysterious messages from beyond?" I say melodically, mocking her.

"Do you think she was messing with you?"

"I don't know. She said my father was ready to join my mother."

"That's not difficult to believe." He carefully measures my reaction.

"Everything else she said was very cryptic."

"Did anything bring you comfort?"

A small ceramic bird figurine on the end table tremors ever so slightly and moves no more than a fraction of an inch. Its movement was so subtle that I would never have known it moved if I hadn't been staring at it. Sawyer averts his eyes to where my gaze is locked. "Grace?"

The sound of his voice interrupts my thoughts. "I think I want to go to work today."

"Are you sure?" he asks, surprised.

"Yeah. I think I need to get back to normal. Keep my mind busy."

"Doing creative things will probably help you recharge. I'm not going to lie. I have to go in for training today, and I'd feel a lot better knowing you're not hanging out here by yourself."

"It's settled then. I'll go get ready."

Sawyer kisses me on the lips. "I've got to leave now. You have a great day, and call me later."

"I will."

"Come home if you start feeling tired. You don't have to start back full days if you're not up to it."

I feel agitated and snap at him. "Give it a rest, Sawyer! I just buried my father. I'm not battling cancer. I'll be fine."

He flashes me a heated look. "I'm just worried about you." He closes the door forcefully, and I know I've upset him. It's not how I'd like for him to start his day.

I take a deep breath and turn the doorknob at the front entrance. The small bell jingles, signalling someone has entered the store. "I'll be right with you," Sara yells from the back room.

She stops in her tracks when she sees me. "Grace! What are you doing here?"

"I'm coming to work."

"So soon? Honey, you can take as much time as you need."

"What I need is to get back to work and get out of my head."

She throws her arms around me. "If you're ready, I'm thrilled to have you back."

"I'm ready."

"How is Sawyer? Has he been taking good care of you?"

"Too good."

"That's a good thing, Grace."

I take an emotional breath. "I'm afraid that he's doing such a good job of taking care of me that when he's gone, I won't take care of myself."

"What do you mean...when he's gone? Where's he going?" Understanding suddenly comes to her. "Oh, honey. You're afraid that you're going to depend on him so much that if anything happens to him, you're going to feel like your father did after your mom passed."

I shrug. "I wasn't very nice to Sawyer this morning."

"Don't you dare try and push that boy away."

"I need to do something nice for *him*, for a change."

"Well, let's discuss what that might be while we take a quick inventory and order some merchandise."

"Was I gone that long?"

"Less than a week, but it felt like a year. I need your brains."

I fully immersed myself in work and creative processes. When I left work, I had a plan for how to make it up to Sawyer.

"Grace?" he calls out, cautiously navigating the hallway. "Why is the house in darkness?"

"Hi!" I greet him at the entrance to the kitchen.

"What's going on? Is the power out? The number for the electrician is on the fridge."

"No, the power isn't out. Come with me."

Without hesitation, he takes my hand, and I guide him through the side door and into the side garden. I spent an hour lighting candles and hanging twinkle lights from the trees. "Did you do all this yourself?" he asks, impressed.

"I did."

"What's the occasion?"

I lead him to the table where I've prepared his favourite grilled steak and mushroom dinner. "No occasion. Just an apology for being bitchy this morning."

We sit across from each other at the small round patio table.

"Well, if those are loaded baked potatoes, I accept your apology."

"Thank you. If only I had known it would be that easy."

"Hey, it's been a difficult week. You're entitled to have an off day."

"Thank you for all you do. I know you're just looking out for me."

"That was part of our pact, right?"

"If you start talking about spitting in hands right now, I swear I will stab you with your steak knife."

Sawyer slides his cutlery away from my reach. "There's my girl. Welcome back."

Sawyer forgave me in the candlelit garden. He continued to forgive me on the stairs and against the wall in the hallway. But there is nothing sexier than finding him standing at the stove cooking breakfast the next morning. His pyjama pants hang on his hips and tempt me with a teasing view of his magnificent gluteus maximus. I wrap my arms around him from behind and brush my lips across the bare skin of his back.

"Be careful what you start," he warns.

"That is neither a threat nor a deterrent." I let go of him and reach for a mug from the cupboard.

"Tea's in the pot."

"You're the perfect man. Marry me."

Sawyer freezes, and I immediately regret saying it. He turns to give me a daunting look.

"I was just teasing."

"Well, then, wouldn't you have been surprised if I said yes?"

"That's absurd. You wouldn't say yes."

His brow creases. "I wouldn't?"

"You don't want to get married." He looks confused and I pause. "*Do* you want to get married?"

"I think I would. If the right girl came along."

I become tongue-tied, and he grins.

"When the time is right, of course."

"Of course." How did I get myself into this?

Sawyer places two plates on the table, and I join him with my tea.

"How was work?" he asks between bites.

"I'm glad I went back. It kept my mind busy."

"How about you? How are things with your new job?"

"Training has been a bit of a grind. Now I have more availability I can push through it faster."

"That's good to hear. It was nice of them to be so flexible with you, considering you just started."

"I guess I was their best candidate, so they were happy to give me some time. And, Ben is just finishing up a project, so he's committed to starting our restorations in a few weeks."

"Do you have ideas, or are you still figuring that part out?"

"He thinks there's a few structural issues we have to fix, then all new electrical and plumbing."

"That sounds expensive."

"I might need a side hustle to pay for everything."

"I can start paying rent. Tell me what you think is fair."

"Absolutely not. Sorry, Grace. I wasn't fishing for that."

"It's only fair I share in the expenses since I'm living here."

"You're a guest."

I lower my brow.

"Well, not a guest. You're my girlfriend who lives here currently. But I'm not charging you rent."

I shrug. "Okay, I'll buy the groceries."

He growls in frustration. "Have you heard from the insurance company yet?"

"They're waiting for the official fire investigation to be filed. He said they'll have contractors come in and secure the site so it meets safety bylaws, and they'll let me know within a few weeks how much the claim will be approved for."

"They don't move too quickly, do they?"

"I don't know if this is normal or not."

I clear the plates from the table. "Can I ask a favour?"

"Of course."

"Would you take me to the house today?"

His eyes open wide. "Are you sure you want to see that?"

I'm sure I don't. "I need to look for something."

"Sweetheart, there was nothing left."

"There's something I'd like to get from the garden if it wasn't destroyed."

"I can't imagine anything in that garden survived."

"I just have a feeling."

"I really don't think it's a good idea."

I cross my arms, frustrated. "I can drive over there myself, you know."

Sawyer nods, sensing this is not an issue to push me on. "You might want to get dressed."

I look down at my pyjamas. "I've seen people dressed worse at Walmart."

"Suit yourself but I'm getting dressed first."

"I will to. I'll just take a minute."

Sawyer smiles. "I'll wait for you in the truck."

"Are you sure I can't talk you out of this?" Sawyer says concerned. I feel dizzy and lightheaded as we turn onto the street where my parents' home used to stand. Sawyer reaches over and takes hold of my hand. "Grace, are you holding your breath?"

Am I? I concentrate on taking a deep breath and filling my lungs with oxygen.

"It's okay if you change your mind. We can turn around and go home."

"No. I want to do this." Most of the area is still caution taped off. Sawyer drives his truck over the lawn and to the back of the property. I avert my attention away from where the house used to stand. Everything close to the home is charred or covered in ash and waterlogged. I jump out of the truck and sink into the saturated ground. Most of the ivy and flowering bushes hang wilted and dead from the heat of the fire, but just past them, the beautifully preserved garden comes into view.

188

"I can't believe it," Sawyer says, following me to the back of the property. "It's like it was somehow protected."

I walk over to the bench where my father spent most of his hours and sit.

Sawyer sits beside me. "Is this what you came for?"

I stare at the hummingbird feeder. "It is." I wipe the falling tears from my cheeks.

"Let me get it for you."

"Do you think we could take the bench?"

"I'm sure it will fit in the back of the truck."

"You don't mind if I take a few things back to your house?"

He hands me the hummingbird feeder. "Grace, at some point, they're going to come in with heavy equipment, remove the house debris, and likely level the land. If there's anything here you want, let's take it."

Searching through the overgrown gardens for treasures, I feel like a child on an Easter morning egg hunt. I start a small pile of statues and mementos that my parents once enjoyed. "Sawyer, look. These flowers are blooming."

"Dig 'em out. We can transplant them."

"Really?"

He shrugs. "Why not? I've got some boxes in the back of the truck I was going to take to the recycling centre. We can fill them with plants and take them home."

I look past him at an old garden shed. "There might be a shovel in there."

Sawyer tugs on the door, and it opens with some coaxing. There's a loud creaking sound, and I gasp as the entire building leans to one side and then completely collapses. Sawyer jumps back out of the way. When the dust settles, he still holds the door handle. He laughs, and I hold my hand over my heart, relieved he wasn't hurt.

"You know what?" He tosses the handle into the pile of rubble and brushes the dust off his clothes. "This is something that Jake and Ben can help me do later."

He loads the bench and the silly little statues into the back of the truck, making sure they're secure. I keep the hummingbird feeder in the front seat with me. "Thank you," I say when we're halfway home.

"For what?"

"Letting me bring this stuff back to your house. When it first happened, all I could think about was that I had lost everything. Now I feel like I've got some of my parents back. It's like they're no longer erased from the world."

"Grace, they will never be erased. They'll always live on in your heart and your memories."

I grip the hummingbird feeder tighter. "I know, and I have no idea why I'm feeling so sentimental over a garden gnome with worn-out paint, a chipped ear and missing all of the fingers on his one hand."

"Not all of them. There's still one left. And really...one is all you need."

I purse my lips, trying not to react, but I can't help myself. I lose my self-control and burst into laughter as we pull up to the farmhouse.

I unload my garden statues as if they were priceless archeological artifacts. When they're safely out of the way, I watch Sawyer lift the bench off the back of the truck. He catches me looking and smiles. I take a long, appreciative look at his broad shoulders and chiselled muscles.

"Where would you like the bench?"

"In the garden at the end of the pathway? Is that too much trouble?"

"None at all. I want you to consider this as your place, too."

His purely masculine body glistens from exertion in the heat of the afternoon. I'm mesmerized by every movement and every muscle as he moves heavy items around the garden. I have never met a man who ignites the fire inside me as much as Sawyer Kelly does. Something comes over me. Something unexpected. Something almost feral. I walk toward him and, taking hold of his shirt, pull him against my chest. Unsure of what's going on, he resists at first, but when he sees my lips, he surrenders to a passionate kiss. His strong hands on my body magnify my sensory level a million times, sending flashes of heat and energy through me. Sawyer responds, pushing his pelvis forward and making me aware of his growing need.

We stumble through the yard, kissing each other, trying to make our way to the house. Stopping at the truck, he lifts me onto the hood, and I pull him between my widespread knees with pure aching need and stoking desire a notch higher.

"House. NOW!" he growls, lowering me to my feet.

I waste no time getting to the front door and pushing it open. When I reach the stairs, he grabs my arm and stops me dead. I pivot toward him, startled. "That's too far away. I want you now." He lifts me effortlessly, takes two strides into the living room, and lowers me to the floor.

His lips burn a trail of fire down my neck. Strong hands caress my breasts, hungrily searching for bare skin and failing. A low feral growl escapes from his lips, and he grips both sides of my blouse and forcefully pulls it apart as if he were tearing a piece of paper. Buttons bounce and ricochet across the room with force. I barely catch my breath as he rids me of my pants just as quickly.

Stripping himself bare, he climbs on top of my body, power emanating tautly through his biceps. I push my hips against him, silently pleading with him to sate the ache there. He presses his lips to mine as he grants me my wish, swallowing my moans of pleasure.

Recovering from the passion, we lay motionless on the hard floor. Sawyer grabs a corner of the throw blanket from the couch and tugs it to the ground. He grunts as he pulls it over us, and I barely have enough energy to let out a small laugh. Snuggling up behind me, I feel the warmth of his lips on my shoulder, and then I feel him trace the image of my tattoo with his finger. "Your tattoo is beautiful," he says.

My eyes flutter open. I haven't thought of it as beautiful in many years. Instead, it's been a constant reminder of noncommittal and short-lived romances.

"Why a hummingbird?"

I shrug, not wanting to answer. "Why not?"

"Fair enough." He forces me to roll over on my back so he can see my face. "It's time to prove that two people fit in that tub."

Chapter Seventeen

"Good morning!" I call out when Jake and Ben get out of their truck.

"Morning! We dug out all the plants that looked healthy."

"Thank you for doing that. I wish there was something I could do to repay your kindness."

"Keep Sawyer happy. That's payment enough," Ben says.

Jake starts taking pots off the trailer. "Our friend, Mason, owns a landscaping business. He's going to come by later and put these in the ground."

Ben walks toward me with a card. "Give some thought to where you want them, and then give him a call. If you don't have any preferences, he'll just do his thing."

"Sawyer is out on a rescue call, so I'll try to figure it out on my own."

They hop back into the truck and wave as they turn around on the dirt driveway. I take a quick inventory of the plants that are there. My parents had a beautiful garden, but I had nothing to do with that. I wouldn't know the first thing about planting, or plants, or gardens. I walk down the pathway to the cement bench and search for garden plans on my phone. Hours pass, and I feel like I still have no idea what to do with the endless buckets of rescued flora.

I need a break. As I walk to the house to get a refreshment, I dial the number on Mason's card. When I go to voicemail, I let him know it's me calling and tell him to go ahead and do his thing when he has time.

I exit the side door and fill a bucket with water to keep them moist until they can be transplanted. When I turn the corner of the house, Sawyer's truck is in the driveway. I look around for him, but I don't see him. I dump a small amount of water in each pot, and I think I can hear his voice in the distance. I walk down the pathway toward the back garden, and I can hear him much clearer now. With his phone to his ear, he paces back and forth between two outbuildings, laser-focused on the conversation. I hear something that catches my attention, so I step back so as not to be seen. I hope the good Lord will forgive me for eavesdropping. From Sawyer's side of the conversation, it appears the caller is his old employer in Alberta.

"So, you're offering me a position on the board of directors? And exactly how much does that pay?" He whistles. "That's hard to turn down."

My heart sinks.

"And when would you want me to start?"

Feeling devastated, I walk back to the house. I've completely lost the desire to finish watering flowers. When I walk into the kitchen, every cabinet door is open. I curse. "Don't mess with me today!" I say aloud. "I'm not in the mood."

"Who are you talking to?" Sawyer asks as he enters the room. I jump. He pauses and looks around at the open cupboards. "What's going on? Were you looking for something?"

"Nope. They were like this when I came in."

He helps me close them. "That's odd."

"Mmhmm. One of many odd things."

He quirks a brow. "What do you mean?"

I drop my hands heavily to my side. "Do you mean to tell me you've never wondered what the explanation is for all the weird stuff that goes on here?"

"Like?"

"Oh, I don't know. Like footsteps in the middle of the night. Shadows. Things moving on their own."

"I just figured it's an old house, and things shift."

I hold my hand on my forehead in disbelief. "That's exactly what my dad would have said."

He shakes his head. "Never mind that now, I have something important I need to talk to you about." His phone screeches to life, and he curses. "I'm sorry, I've got another call, but I promise this won't go on for much longer." He kisses me on the lips. "I'll talk to you later." He rushes off, totally unaware of my distress.

My heart aches thinking about him moving back to Alberta. He seemed so convincing when he talked about finally coming home to stay. I wanted to believe him. Happily-ever-after is not in my cards. Happily-never-after seems to be my destiny. This is why I've been so reluctant to lean on anyone. When you lean on people, you depend on them. Now, I'll have to get used to doing things on my own again. I had been thinking that perhaps this could be my future home with Sawyer. Now it appears I need to call the insurance company and find out when my house can be rebuilt because I need a place to live. When Sawyer returns home, he quietly steps into the room. I pretend I'm asleep.

I slip out of bed in the early morning to investigate a strange buzzing sound outside the window. When I find nothing that explains the odd occurrence, I decide to dress and go to work.

Sara opens the door and cautiously peeks in. "You're early."

"I couldn't sleep."

"Is everything okay?"

"Fine."

She folds her arms across her chest and tilts her head.

"Okay, I'm not fine. But I don't want to talk about it."

"Honey, I can handle things here if you need more time off to see a grief counsellor."

"No, that's not it."

A voice hollers from the other room. "Aunt Sara! I've brought by those pieces you wanted."

"You go and look after that. I'm fine. Honest."

I close my door and throw myself into my work. I can't concentrate. I hold my head in my hands, trying to still my thoughts, when my office door swings open, and Sawyer sticks his head in.

"What are you doing here?" I ask, feeling agitated.

“You left early, and I didn’t get to talk to you. I thought we could go out for lunch.”

“I’m sorry, I can’t. I’m too busy.”

“Too busy for lunch? Unheard of.”

“I can’t.” I look away.

“Oh,” he says, looking wounded. “I won’t bother you. I’ll see you at home.”

Now I feel like a bitch. “Sorry. It’s just busy now, and I’ve got a lot of things to do.”

He concedes. “Busy is good.”

“Yes, it is.” I need to end this awkward conversation. I get to my feet and walk toward the door. “I’ll see you later.”

He pauses, looking like he has something to say. I do everything I can to avoid eye contact. If I look into his eyes, I’m done. Frustrated, he turns and leaves.

“What was that about?” Sara asks, standing in the doorway shortly after.

“Nothing.”

“It sure seemed like something was going on.”

“Were you spying on me?”

“Um, no. It’s a small shop, and there’s no privacy here.”

“For once, mind your own business.” I get up and close the door in her face. I sit in my office until I’m sure the store is closed, and Sara is gone.

When I get to Sawyers, it’s nearly dusk. I walk down the pathway and sit on the bench in the garden, trying to sort out my thoughts. I can’t bring myself to go into the house just yet.

Sawyer comes looking for me. "What are you doing out here?"

"I needed some fresh air."

"I've called you a few times. I noticed your car was here, so I figured this is where I'd find you."

"You found me."

"Rough day?"

"I spoke with the Insurance company."

Sawyer sits beside me. "What did they say?"

"It's going to be about two years before they can start to rebuild."

"That's a long time."

"I'm going to start looking for somewhere to live."

"What?" he asks, confused. "I meant to talk to you about it officially, but I thought you would live here *with me*."

I do everything in my power to hold back tears. "Two years is too long."

His jaw tenses. "What's going on, Grace?"

"Nothing."

He swats at the menacing intruders in the air. "I don't know what's going on in your head, but can we talk about it inside? The bugs are getting thick out here."

I purposely walk two feet away to avoid any body contact between us. I follow him into the house, but I'm tired, and I want this day to be done. "I'm going to get ready for bed."

He stands at the bottom of the stairs and watches me make my way to the second floor. I hold my breath, hoping he doesn't come after me.

I draw out the time I need in the bathroom, trying to avoid him. When I'm done, he's waiting for me in the bedroom.

"Can we talk now?" He asks, reaching for my hand.

I pull it out of his grip and pick up some of my things.

"Is this because I'm being constantly called away for emergency calls? I talked to the organizer today and reduced my available hours until they can recruit more volunteers. Then they'll take me off the roster."

It's kind of hard to volunteer from Alberta. My heart is aching, so I need to put a stop to this. "I just think it's better if I sleep in the other room."

He tries to hide a wounded expression. "Is that what you want?"

I nod.

He rakes his hands through his hair, trying to maintain his composure. "Okay. I said you could stay here, *no strings* attached. If it would make you feel more comfortable, you're welcome to the spare bedroom." He looks completely defeated. "Just tell me. Did I do something wrong?"

"No."

"Why does it feel like I kicked your puppy or something?"

"It's just better this way. This was a mistake."

He becomes frustrated: "*We* are *not* a mistake."

"Stop with the games, Sawyer. No version of this story ends with us riding off into the sunset together."

"Why not?"

"Because. It's been ten years since college, and I'm not the same girl."

He takes two giant steps toward me. "You *are* the same girl," he insists.

I shake my head as he reaches for me. I'm so guarded I feel my body stiffen at his touch.

He pauses and gentles his grip. "You've been through a traumatic experience. You're scared and feeling overwhelmed. I get that but don't push me away. Stay in the other room tonight if you want. But we're going to talk tomorrow."

As if it were a sign, the door to the other bedroom slams shut at the end of the hallway. We both turn to look.

Sawyer raises his brow. "Sounds like you won't be alone. Are you sure you don't want to change your mind?"

I look down the hallway, hesitant and frightened.

He grabs his phone and a pillow. "Never mind. You stay in this room. I'll sleep down the hall."

Chapter Eighteen

I have a very restless sleep. Every time I open my eyes, I envision my life alone after Sawyer leaves for Alberta. I have no family left, and I'm sure I've lost my only friend and business partner after yesterday. It's better if I put sentiment and emotions aside. If I'm going to survive a breakup with Sawyer, I need to squash any feelings I have and toughen up.

I heard Sawyer leave for training at the crack of dawn, and it hurt my heart that he didn't come in and kiss me goodbye. But then, why would he? I drew the line in the sand last night and he has too much integrity to try and force me to do something I don't want to do.

There's a strange sound outside my window. A few days ago, I was convinced there was a beehive in the wall or in the roof. Sawyer had someone come out to check, but they couldn't find anything. After the past few days, it wouldn't surprise me if it was a plague of locusts.

I get dressed and follow the buzzing sound down the pathway to the back of the property. The sun gently peaks over the horizon, lighting the garden with a radiant glow. I feel empty. I feel numb. I've lost everything, and I've lost *everyone*. The closer I get to the garden, the further away the sound seems to get until it suddenly stops altogether. I'm feeling way too dismal to sit on the cement bench today. Looking around me at all the statues that were brought from my parent's house only makes me feel more disenchanted with the garden.

Walking back toward the house, I realize I didn't see the calico cat around this morning. I spend time looking for her, but in all honesty, I'm just avoiding going to work.

I finally gather the courage to drive into town. I sit in my car, stalling and trying to think of what I'm going to say. I open the door to the main entrance of the store and stick my head in, waiting to gauge her reaction. Sara looks up from a display and pauses.

"Hi," I say sheepishly. "Is it okay if I come in?"

"You own half the shop. I couldn't keep you out if I wanted to." She turns away so she's not looking at me.

I wrinkle my nose. "I wouldn't blame you if you wanted to."

She sighs and places the inventory on the table then looks at me and frowns. "Get in here."

I take a deep breath, feeling relief, and push the door open.

"I'm sorry, Sara."

"Me too. We're business partners, but I thought we were also friends."

"We are. I mean I hope we still can be. I was freaking out, and I reacted without thinking."

"Are you going to tell me why you were freaking out?"

"I'd rather not."

"Does this have something to do with what we were talking about the other day?"

"No."

"Did Sawyer do something wrong?"

I pause, and she raises a brow.

"Why were you treating him like that?"

I shrug my shoulders, feeling ashamed. "I'm scared."

"For the love of God, Grace. Spit it out."

"I think Sawyer is planning to move back to Alberta."

"What? I don't believe it."

"I heard him on the phone."

"Really? You overheard him?"

"Yes."

"Did you ask him about what you overheard?"

"No."

She drops her hands heavily on the display top, frustrated. "Have you seen any Hallmark movies? This is obviously a case of misheard information."

"There was no misheard information. I heard it all clearly. Until I walked away."

Sara puts her hand on her forehead. "You're killing me. So, you heard part of a conversation, and without talking to him, you're going to push him aside and throw away everything…" she cocks her head to the side and gives me an inquisitive look. "For what reason?"

"To protect myself."

"BEN!!!!" Sara screams.

My eyes open wide as the mountainous man barrels out of the back room, ducking as he narrowly misses banging his head on the low doorway threshold. I had no idea he was here.

"Hi, Grace," he says, surprised.

"Sorry, I was outside helping one of the vendors unload. What's up?"

I hope Sara understands my silent plea not to tell Ben.

"Can you watch the store for an hour? There's something Grace and I need to do."

"Sure. I have to meet a client for a final inspection this afternoon, so as long as you're back just after lunch."

"Thank you, we won't be gone long."

"Is everything okay?" he asks reluctantly while narrowing his eyes.

"Right as rain," I confirm.

Ben looks at Sara. "Why don't I believe her?"

"Because she's lying."

I close my eyes and show a pained expression.

"Well, let's go." Sara places her hand on my shoulder and nudges me toward the door.

"Where are we going?" I ask as we exit out into the parking lot.

"Just get in the car."

We've only been on the road for a few minutes, and based on our route, I know exactly where she's taking me. I sit silently, afraid to open my mouth. When Sara drives between the cement pillars at the cemetery gate, the sky is blue and welcoming, in complete contrast to the last time I was here. Birds sing as we walk the path to the graveside, and the sun warms my face as if trying to erase the memories of the harsh punishment of the driving rain.

The ground has dried out, and the grass is trying to grow beneath our feet as we walk, but the sight of the loose dirt covering the grave brings back the pain of how recent his passing was. It's peaceful here, with no traffic noises and no interruptions. There's a magnificent view of the Hills of the Headwaters region for as far as you can see. My dad loved it here. When he came to visit my mom, he would stay for hours.

"Why did you bring me here?" I finally find the nerve to ask her.

"I want you to tell them."

"Tell them what?"

"You stand here and tell your parents why you're going to walk away from a chance to have the kind of love they always wanted you to find."

"Sara," I begin to plead.

She holds her hand in the air. "Nope. You tell them. I'm going to stand over there and give you some privacy."

I stand alone at the grave, staring at the tombstone and feeling awkward. I scratch my head, wondering how to do this. Can they read my thoughts, or do I have to speak them aloud?

"Out loud!" Sara yells as if she can read my mind.

"I don't know where to start."

"Start with...I'm in love with Sawyer Kelly," she suggests.

Why does that word evoke so many complicated emotions? "Dad, you were right. I think I've always been in love with Sawyer. I didn't know it until he came back to town and turned my life upside down." I take a tissue out of my pocket, preparing for an emotional purge. "Mom, I miss you so much. I tried to become the strong woman you raised me to be. When I'm around Sawyer, I let my guard down. I didn't know I needed to lean on someone to heal my emotional soul. It feels good to let him look after me sometimes. It feels really good. So good it's scary. There's a chance he might be leaving town, so I feel like ending things with him now is the right thing to do because I don't want to live the rest of my life feeling broken-hearted."

Sara walks back to the grave and stands at my side.

"What if Sawyer is your one great love?"

I shrug. "I will never know."

"What's keeping you here?"

I sniffle and wipe away a tear. "What do you mean?"

"If he's considering going back to Alberta, why can't you go with him?"

"Because everything I have is here."

She gives me a sympathetic smile. "Honey, the only thing you have here right now is Sawyer."

I pause and think about it. My parents are gone, and the house I grew up in is gone. "What about you and the store?"

"You'll never be able to get rid of me. No matter what province you live in. As for the store, you can sell your share, or we can branch out and open another store in Alberta."

208

There are so many thoughts whirling around in my head. "I never thought about that."

"Do you love him?"

"Yes."

"Then it's worth taking the risk."

"If he wanted me to go to Alberta with him, why didn't he say something."

Sara purses her lips and widens her eyes. "Did you give him the chance?"

I look down, feeling regretful. "I didn't. He said he had something important to talk to me about, and I panicked into flight mode."

"What would your parents tell you to do?"

I hold my hands over my face before taking a deep breath and dropping my arms to my side. "They'd tell me to go."

She smiles, and her eyes start to sparkle. "Now, do you understand why I brought you here?"

I nod.

Sara reaches up and caresses my arms. "My parents have been dead for many years, and I still go to their grave and talk to them when I'm struggling. Even though they no longer walk this earth, they have a strong influence on me."

A small brown bunny hops along beside us as we make our way to the car.

"If I'm in Alberta, I won't be able to visit their grave."

"Only their physical bodies are buried here, Grace. You can talk to their spirits from wherever you are."

"I want to believe wherever I go, they'll be with me."

"If you believe, they will be."

I feel a bit lighter as Sara drives back to the store, but I'm still not one hundred percent convinced. "What if he doesn't want me to go with him?"

Sara smiles as she glances at me. "What if he does?"

"We're back," She hollers to Ben. "I told you we wouldn't be long."

He ducks as he comes out of the back room. "You just missed Sawyer; he came by to talk to Grace."

"Where is he now?"

"He had to go back to training. He only had a few minutes for lunch."

I frown. "What did he tell you?"

"That something upset you, and he has no idea what he did or how to fix it."

"She's going to fix it," Sara assures him.

"I'll talk to him tonight," I promise.

"Is everything okay?" he asks, concerned.

My heart squeezes uncomfortably in my chest. "I don't know. I wish I had all the answers, but I don't right now."

Ben looks almost as crushed as Sawyer did last night.

"Well, whatever it is. I hope you can work it out. You two belong together." He walks toward the door and turns one last time to wave goodbye.

"I'm going to get going as well."

Sara throws her arms around me. "Everything will work out the way it's meant to be. Just be open to new and scary things."

I pull out onto the highway and find myself drawn to the exit that takes me north. I follow my impulse and head out of town. I drive for almost an hour until I find myself in the middle of Mennonite country. Their properties are easily distinguished by the meticulously maintained farms and homes with green metal roofing. I pull off the road and get out of my car to look at the goods at a farm stand at the end of a driveway.

Three children between the ages of ten and twelve are keeping watch over the stand. The two girls are busy reading and the younger boy is playing with a frog in the grass.

"Good afternoon," I say cheerfully as one of the girls acknowledges me.

"Hi. The prices are written on the baskets."

"Thank you, I see that." I want to tell them that they aren't charging enough. At the market in town, the vendors get more than double what they're asking for.

"Did you help grow these vegetables?" I ask the young boy when he wanders over to see what's going on. He nods and hides behind his sister.

"We all help. Everyone has a job," the young girl says proudly.

"Well, I'm looking for some fresh vegetables to have with my dinner, and these are the finest I've seen." I put a basket of beans and a head of lettuce to the side.

"Is that everything?" The older of the two girls asks in a rather mature fashion.

"Unless you've got some raisin bread, that's all I need for today."

"Joseph, run to the house and ask Momma if she has any raisin bread."

He takes off running, and I feel bad. "He didn't need to disturb her."

The girls give me the total and dump the veggies into a brown paper bag. I realize that I need cash. "Just a minute, I need to get money from the car." I scour every compartment and cup holder, looking for spare change. One last place to look, I flip open the centre console, and for a moment, I'm frozen. I had completely forgotten that he gave it to me and asked me to keep it safe. I reach for my father's wallet and flip it open to find what I'm looking for. After sliding out a couple of bills, I stick the wallet in my pocket and walk back to pay.

As I approach the stand, a young woman walks toward me. "Good day!" she says with a bright smile.

"Good day!"

"Thank you for stopping. This is for you. Joseph said you were asking."

She hands me a loaf wrapped in butcher paper. I can feel the warmth through the paper and I know it's not long been out of the oven.

"How much do I owe you?"

212

"Nothing. It's my gift to you on such a beautiful day."

Now I feel bad for not buying more vegetables.

"You're extremely kind. Thank you." Before walking away, I drop what's left of the change into a mason jar on the vegetable stand. The little girl smiles at me. "When you get a chance, do something extra nice for your momma."

She nods. "I will."

I pull away from the farm and start my journey home. Traffic builds as I get closer to town. The smell of cinnamon and raisins fills the air and makes me hungry. Eating has been the last thing on my mind for the past few days.

Chapter Nineteen

When I arrive at the house, I take the vegetables inside and put them in the fridge. Then I unwrap the raisin bread on the counter and cut myself a rather thick slice. The butter melts against the still-warm loaf as I spread it evenly across the top. In one bite, I understand why the country baked fresh bread was his favourite. I take it with me, eating it as I walk along the pathway to the garden. The sun has begun to set, and brilliant orange rays of light pierce through the spaces between tree branches like bolts of lightning on the horizon.

An emerald-green hummingbird whizzes past my ear and hovers at the feeder we brought from the old house. Sawyer took the time to find the perfect place for it in the garden. The absence of the midday sun cools the air. I pull my sweater around me and feel the wallet in my pocket. I pull it out and sit on the bench, holding it tightly in my hand.

"Can I join you?"

I look up to see Sawyer approaching. "Yes."

"I saw your car at the shop and stopped in to talk."

"Ben told me."

"What are you doing out here? It's getting late."

"You must be exhausted. You left really early."

"I am. Did you get any sleep?"

"Not much. You?"

"None." He sits down beside me. "What have you got there?"

"I found my dad's wallet in the console of my car." I flip it open and start to look through several photos that are worn and creased. "These are the only pictures left in this world of him and my mom." Tears stream down my face. "The only thing he ever wanted for me was to find that same kind of love for myself."

"What's going on, Grace? Talk to me."

I cover my face. "I can't do this, Sawyer." I get to my feet and start to walk away.

"I'm not letting it go," he says, chasing after me. "I'm not letting you shut me out. Something happened to make you act this way, and I want to know what."

Adrenaline pulses through my veins, and I spin around on the edge of an angry outburst. "Do you want to know what's wrong with me? Let me tell you about the tattoo on my shoulder. I didn't get it to symbolize some magical journey with promises of hope and joy. There is no happily ever after in my story. I'm broken. When I got this tattoo, I thought it was a symbol of hope. Then I discovered the truth. Male hummingbirds put on a fantastic show to attract a female, but they don't commit for life. Once they win her over and get what they want, they move on, leaving her alone. For me, this tattoo is a daily reminder of that."

"Is that what you think I'm going to do?" Sawyer begins to pace like a caged animal, energy radiating off him.

I look away, struggling for control and failing. "That's what every man in my life has done."

"I regret every day that I didn't speak up about my feelings for you. I moved forward with my life, but not for a minute did I move on from you."

I step back, putting some space between us.

"I have spent every moment of the past ten years wishing I was sharing my life with you. Why would I throw that away now that you're back in my life?"

The sincerity in his eyes confuses me. "I heard you on the phone. With your old employer."

His shoulders fall, and he curses under his breath. "I see." He crosses his arms in front of his chest. "So, you were listening to my call?"

"I didn't mean to. I was looking for you and…." I pause, realizing there's no point in defending myself. "I know you're going back to Alberta."

"I'm what?"

"You accepted a new position."

"I did?"

"Wait." I narrow my eyes, puzzled. "Did you take the position?"

He shakes his head. "No, I didn't. I'm not going anywhere. This is home for me now. A home I thought you and I were going to share."

I'm thunderstruck. "I'm confused. After your call, you said there was something important you wanted to talk about."

"There is." He holds out his hand. "Come here, and I'll show you." I hesitate, and he coaxes me further. "Come on." I take his hand, and he walks me to one of the outbuildings, slowly opening the door. "Come in," he encourages. Once I'm in, he closes the door behind me. My eyes take a moment to adjust to the dim light.

I've got an eerie feeling. "You're kind of freaking me out."

"You'll understand in a minute."

"Something just brushed against my leg," I say, alarmed. "Have you got girls chained to the walls out here?"

The light from a small heat lamp barely illuminates the room. He gives me a strange look. "What kind of movies do you watch that would lead you to that conclusion?"

"It's always the ones you expect the least," I joke.

"No women are being held captive in the shed," he assures me. "Just Molly."

I look down at the small calico cat. "Hi, Molly! I was wondering where you got to. I can't believe you named her." I reach down to scratch her head, and she purrs. "What does Molly have to do with your phone call?"

"Absolutely nothing," he growls. "Can you forget about the damn phone call for a minute?"

"Fine, but hurry up. This is getting a little creepy."

"I hadn't seen Molly for a few days, and I was getting worried. When I was hanging your father's hummingbird feeder, I found her in the garden. She was hiding in a hollowed-out tree trunk. She was wet, hungry...and terrified."

"Poor thing. Why do you have her locked out here? Why didn't you bring her into the house?"

There's a tiny squeak from a pile of straw in the corner, and Molly quickly rushes over to it. She stops and turns to look at us proudly and meows. I follow her over and squeal. "Kittens!"

"Six of them," Sawyer confirms. "They couldn't have been more than a few hours old when I found them. I couldn't leave them there."

I'm so confused. I narrow my eyes. "Wait. This was what you wanted to talk about?"

"Yeah. I didn't want to bring them into the house until I asked you if you were ready to be fur parents with me."

"That's it?"

"Well, I thought it was a pretty big thing at the time," he scoffs.

"What about the job offer?"

"I turned it down." He pushes open the door and steps out into the last few moments of the setting sun.

I follow him out of the building. "But I heard you say it was hard to turn down."

"It was. Do you know how much money they were going to offer me?"

"Why didn't you take it then?"

We walk back toward the garden. "There are a lot of reasons. I would have told you about it if you hadn't blindsided me with all this nonsense instead of talking to me."

"You made it sound like something you couldn't pass up."

"Grace. I don't want a position sitting on a board of directors making decisions. I want to be out in the field, making a difference. I just accepted a position that's going to give me what I want out of my career. I'm not going to leave that. The biggest reason I moved back here was *you*."

My head wants to be cautious, but my heart is doing cartwheels. He reaches down, takes my hands in his, and slowly reels me toward him until his arms fully surround me. Strong arms. I lay down my armour and lay my head on his chest, nuzzling in that spot beneath his chin where I belong. I can feel the heavy thumping of his heart.

"I loved you then, and I will always love you, Grace. If you need me to love you hard enough to hold all your broken pieces together, then that's what I'll do. I'm *never* leaving you behind again. You're stuck with me."

I smile. The heartbreak I was feeling has been replaced with renewed feelings of hope.

"I live for that smile."

A hummingbird hangs over Sawyer's head and two more join in at the feeder. I'm astonished at how they're gathering around us at the very moment I need to see them the most.

Sawyer leans back and looks me in the eyes. "Promise me from now on, you'll talk to me instead of overthinking things and jumping to conclusions."

"I promise, I'll try. Old habits die hard."

"We'll work on it together." Holding hands we walk together toward the house. Sawyer pauses and narrows his eyes. "Do you hear that buzzing sound?"

I throw my hands up in the air, exasperated. "Yes! That's the sound I've been hearing it all week."

"What is that?" He walks back toward the bench and stands, watching in awe. I follow him, and my heart begins to race as I experience nature at one of its most beautiful moments.

"Have you ever seen anything like that?" he asks as he digs his phone out of his pocket.

A strange calm washes over me, and I finally feel at peace.

"I count at least ten, or maybe twelve." He takes a video and several pictures to post on his social media. "What do you call a group of hummingbirds? A flock? A gaggle?"

My heart fills with light and hope. "A shimmer." I suddenly understand why my parents felt a connection to them. I smile. "It's called a shimmer," I say, feeling overjoyed.

"You're right," he says, reading his phone. "How did you know that?"

"Someone recently told me about it." Everything she said suddenly makes sense.

"Are we okay now?" He leans his forehead against mine in silent support.

"Very okay."

"I think we should name our farm Hummingbird Hill."

I finally find the courage to say it. "I love you. My dad was right. I have only ever loved you."

Epilogue

Sawyer takes my hand and walks me back to the house. I glance over my shoulder for a few more glimpses of the rare phenomenon that brings with it both an important sign and a compelling message.

"Does this mean you're staying here with me?" Sawyer asks.

"I kind of have to. I'm committed now. We could split the kittens fifty/fifty, but who would get custody of Molly? We'd have to arrange a schedule, plan alternate weekends, and that's entirely too much work."

Sawyer picks me up and throws me over his shoulder. I squeal as he carries me to the house. "You're not going anywhere. This is where you belong. We'll raise a family here and then live our twilight years together in this house."

He lets me slide down his firm, muscular body until my feet hit the floor. "That sounds wonderful to me. Just us and the rest of your ancestors." I lean in for a kiss, but Sawyer pulls away.

"Do you think we could get them to chip in toward the property taxes?"

"I can't believe you just said that."

"Well, it's only fair if they're going to stay here. They should pay something."

As we enter the kitchen, all the cupboard doors swing open at once. We stop dead in our tracks. Holding my breath, I reach for the truck keys on the counter. I pass them to Sawyer and slowly back out of the room. "You're buying dinner." I pivot and bolt out of the house. Sawyer is close on my heels. We're both gasping for air as we jump in the truck and lock the doors.

"What…the ever-loving-fuck?" he asks through panted breaths.

"I think you upset Aunt Vera by suggesting she should pay rent."

He scratches his neck. "Geez, this house has been in my family for hundreds of years. It would break my heart to sell it."

"Then don't. You've been living here for months without even knowing."

"Yes, but now I know."

"I've heard she's harmless. She's just messing with us."

"That sounds like her."

"I don't think she would have left you the house if her plan was to scare you so you didn't want to live here."

He nods and stares down the dirt laneway to the back of the property. "Do you know what I'm thinking?"

"That you're starving?"

"Nope. When Mason is finished with the landscaping, I think the garden would be the perfect place to hold a wedding."

It's the beginning of a new journey. "I think you're right. Molly and her kittens can walk me down the aisle."

Sawyer smiles. "I love you."

"I love you too."

"So, we're really doing this? Building a life here." He nervously glances at the house. "With her?"

Something catches my attention, and I look out the truck window.

Sawyer sees it, too. "Are those white hummingbirds?" He asks, perplexed.

"Yes, two of them. A bonded pair is very unusual." Their white feathers are so pure that they sparkle in the sunlight. Peace surrounds me as I watch them hover, staring at us through the window. Their wings flutter at such a great speed that they create an aura around them that feels ethereal.

"Why are they white? Are they spirits, too?" he asks, concerned.

"I think they might be. I don't know for certain, but there's something familiar about them." I reach for Sawyer's hand and squeeze it reassuringly. "Family spirits. Maybe even guardian angels."

-The End-

About the Author

Tricia Daniels was born and raised in the suburbs of Toronto, Ontario. 30 years ago, she moved to a small town in Dufferin County where she raised three sons as a single mother. The happily-ever-after she thought she would never have took her by surprise when she met her one great love, later in life. Love changes everything and Tricia Daniels strives to bring you love stories you can relate to.

For all my social media information and information about some of my other stories, please use the QR code below.